THE GHOST OF SUZUKO

Vincent Brault

THE GHOST
OF SUZUKO

Translated from the French by
Benjamin Hedley

QC FICTION

Revision: Peter McCambridge
Proofreading: Daniel J. Rowe, Guil Lefebvre
Book design: Folio infographie
Cover & logo: Maison 1608 by Solisco
Cover art: Getty Images
Fiction editor: Peter McCambridge

ISBN 978-1-77186-276-9 pbk; 978-1-77186-277-6 epub;
978-1-77186-278-3 pdf

Legal Deposit, 2nd quarter 2022
Bibliothèque et Archives nationales du Québec
Library and Archives Canada

Published by QC Fiction, an imprint of Baraka Books
Printed and bound in Québec

TRADE DISTRIBUTION & RETURNS
Canada - UTP Distribution: UTPdistribution.com
United States & World - Independent Publishers Group: IPGbook.com

Société
de développement
des entreprises
culturelles
Québec

Financé par le gouvernement du Canada
Funded by the Government of Canada | Canada

We acknowledge the financial support for translation and
promotion of the Société de développement des entreprises
culturelles (SODEC), the Government of Québec tax credit for
book publishing administered by SODEC, the Government of
Canada, and the Canada Council for the Arts.

"The blank empty space unfolds, containing nothing within. It holds nothing more than an expanse of desolate absence."
Hiromi Kawakami, translated by Allison Markin Powell

Strange Weather in Tokyo

1

"Sorry, I'm not sure if I'm in the right place... Ono Ayumi invited me, but... I forgot my phone... so if I remember right..."

Voices and electronic music inside the house.

"You're in the right place, come in! Ayumi'll be happy to see you."

"Yeah?"

"Of course she will! I'll go get her."

I take my shoes off in the entryway. Press my palms hard against my eyes. Burns a little. So strange to be back here. I breathe in. Breathe out slowly. Breathe in again. I'll be alright.

I've been to Ayumi's maybe once or twice before. Hypnotic music. Takamasa. Maybe twenty people in the living room. Three girls in metallic one-piece suits standing in front of a low, curved, narrow couch. Cold lighting. Makes your skin glassy. Polished cement floor. Exposed cement wall. Cracks and holes. Two long rectangular windows overlooking an inner courtyard. A few people I know here. Black nylon socks. Loose beige blouses. Grey shirts. Belted skirts above the navel. Crimson jackets. Fine straight leg pants and tights. I stick out like a sore thumb. And not just because of the jeans and tatty brown wool sweater I'm wearing. I feel out of place. I did have a shower this morning but that was before two planes and two bus rides. Hour and a half on a bike too.

All because of the earthquake.

Helmet still in my hands. Orange, loud like the three girls in one-pieces. Not as chic, though. People greet me. Smile at me. And turn around then, whisper things I only half hear.

"He was with Suzuko..."

"...I didn't know he was back..."

"I thought he looked different..."

"...everyone knew Suzuko..."

"I wonder what they did with her head..."

Huge urge to run for my life suddenly but then someone asks me what the helmet's for.

"Uhh... oh... It's because of the earthquake, caught me by surprise, you didn't feel it?"

"Eeeh! No, not at all!"

He laughs.

"I forgot what they were like. I ran out quickly, forgot my phone, wallet, keys, and rode here from Sumida."

"Whoa! That's twenty kilometres from here!"

"I had no choice. Luckily I have a good memory, didn't have much trouble finding Ayumi's hou–"

Her winter complexion. Prominent cheekbones.

"Ayumi! I didn't know if I'd make it here in time, but..."

"I'm so happy to see you, Vincent."

She throws herself into my arms.

"Time flies. Three months already."

"Yeah."

She takes a step back. The paleness of her legs. Their reflection on the polished cement floor.

"It's good that you're here... really."

Then she buries her face in her hands. Laughing or crying?

"You ok, Ayumi?"

"I'm ok."

She takes a deep breath and then forces herself to smile.

"Did you fly in today?"

"Yeah, a few hours ago. I thought– "

"Stop. Tell me later! Let's get you a drink first!"

Ono Ayumi spent her twenties in London, study-ing art history. She's 36, 37 now, maybe, but if you met her on the street you'd swear she was ten years younger.

She runs a contemporary art gallery on the ground floor of the most magnificent building in Ginza, a skyscraper so delicate-looking you'd think it'd go flying off if the wind picked up. The first time I set foot in the place was for Li Yi-Fan's vernissage.

6:51. Red numbers. White sheets. The edge of the bed, a steep cliff. No one on my left. Or on my right. It's... ah yes... the party... Ayumi's. Still here, I guess. Her room. Morning? Evening? No idea. Jet lag. The house. Dead quiet. My jeans on the floor at the foot of the bed. My t-shirt folded on the night table. My body heavy. I want to go back to sleep but I force myself to get up, put my jeans on, my t-shirt. It smells wonderfully fresh. I bury my face in it. The smell of Japanese washing detergent. It's all coming back to me now. I leave the room.

"Ayumi?"

Not in the living room or the garden or the kitchen. Nothing out of place. Not a single thing. I go back to the bedroom. I need a shower, desperately, but I make the bed first. A small piece of paper, on the floor. It must have fallen off the night table when I flicked my t-shirt.

Dear Vincent,

You're sleeping and I dare not wake you, but it's 2 in the afternoon and I have to leave. I have an appointment at the gallery, and I'm going out with friends afterwards. Please, make yourself at home and feel free to use the shower. I cleaned your t-shirt and sweater. No need to thank me, I had a load to clean anyways. I left your t-shirt beside the bed (you probably already found it). Your sweater is on the clothesline in the garden. I hope it's dry when you wake up.

In case you forgot... I just want to remind you that last night (or very early this morning rather) you agreed to come talk about Suzuko at the gallery.

We'll be expecting you Wednesday at 3, then. I hope I wasn't being too pushy. You don't have to prepare anything, really, it's just a small, informal gathering, I'm only inviting people you know. We'll chat before then, I'm sure. Anyways, welcome back to Tokyo. Have a great day. And see you soon.

Ayumi

I head straight for the shower. The bathroom fills with steam. My lungs too. My brain. Does me well. But it's weird... I don't remember Ayumi inviting me to talk about Suzuko at the gallery.

Must be the fatigue. The jet lag. The alcohol. Woke up. In her bed. Couch looks hard as a rock. Did we sleep together? I don't think so. Just passed out from the exhaustion, most likely. Jet lag. Alcohol. Yes. Must be it. She slept curled up on the narrow couch. Or not. Or a little. Maybe. Otherwise I'd remember something. I have to get out of the shower. Floor's too cold. But the doorman in my building leaves at 10 p.m. I have to get home before that, else nobody'll be there to let me in. And I'd be overstaying my welcome if I spent another night at Ayumi's. Oh, Pavle's, I could go there. He lives in Sumida too. Not too far from my place. But he doesn't know I'm back. So nice in the shower. So cold outside. 6 degrees, at most. Not a fiber of my being wants to ride home on my bike. Night. Forever. The shower. The steam. The heat. Forever.

I close the door behind me and immediately I miss the comforts of Ayumi's place. I hop on my bicycle. It's gonna take a while. Raining. Kind of. The drops don't fall, they're stuck in the air, floating, forming an endless wall of mist which swallows me up. I ride. First, a narrow road, no sidewalks, lined with two-storey houses. Gropius style. Concrete facades, no obvious windows. Then, a service station at the intersection of a commercial street. I turn right in front of a 7-Eleven and ride until Yoyogi-Hachiman station. I hop off my bike, walk it along the dark, crowded passage under the train tracks. Shibuya. The mist turns to rain. A few people hold magazines open over their heads. Others use a bag or a purse. The people who were really thinking ahead open umbrellas. I ride, orange helmet strapped to my head, alongside an unfamiliar canal. Try to retrace the route I took yesterday. I must've taken a wrong turn somewhere, too soon or too late. I've never been down this way before.

And suddenly there she is, Suzuko, crossing an intersection. I only see the back of her.

Raindrops in the air again, misty, suspended. The feelings of cold, gone. For a moment. Barely long enough to see Suzuko disappear behind a building. Then the rain begins to fall again. I rush to the corner of the street but there's no one in sight. No Suzuko anyway. I keep moving. Eyes peeled. Wandering from street to street. Still nothing. I've veered off track. I'm cold. Must have been someone else. I have to get home. Before ten so the door guy can let me in. I turn right. Left. Lost. Unless... Yeah, looks to me like... Over there... That big road all lit up. The rain is falling harder than before. In thick, frozen lines. My jeans sticking to my thighs. Streams, gushing down the sidewalks, my neck, my back, my legs. The streets shimmering. I'm trembling. Have to get there before 10. Absolutely. But I stop. Wait two minutes at an intersection. Three minutes at another. Hesitating. A sign says 4°C, 7 January 2018. People rushing, running in all directions, impossible to stop any of them. Wouldn't know what to ask them even if I could. Sumida still

21

ten kilometres away. Take the metro they would say but bikes aren't allowed down there. And besides. I have no money on me, no cards. Left everything at home. I keep moving. Have to. Turn left. A long boulevard beneath one of the elevated highways that cross the city. Finally. I ride underneath. Shelter from the heavy rain. Then, to my right, the Mori art museum. Ok. *Mother* by Louise Bourgeois out front. Roppongi. All good now. I know where I am. Finally. Just have to follow the highway eastwards. A hundred metres above me, suspended. Completely silent. There. Shinbashi. And the bar where... Suzuko and I... Suzuko. Again. I haven't stopped thinking about her since I got back. The streets. The rain. The trees. Crows. Cats. Everything reminds me of her. I cross through Ginza, riding along the busiest shopping street. I know this area well. Suzuko's workshop was nearby. I pass the canal. I turn right.

The Sumida River.

I swim from one bank to the other. Sort of. Morishita station. The apartment's just behind. Real close.

I lean my bike against the wall.

I ring.

I wait.

Nobody at the reception desk.

It's past 10 p.m. My wool sweater is stiff. Almost frozen. Body's blue. I sit down in front of the building. Stretch my legs out. Hard, cold ground. My eyes drooping but I don't fall asleep. It's still pouring out and the portico only covers half of me. I'll have to go ring up Pavle. I hope he still lives nearby. A car splashes the sidewalks as it drives by. I'm hungry. I rub my face. My fingers are swollen. Cold cheeks. Numb. The rations box attached to the rack on my bike! Just remembered I have it. Remembered to grab it along with my helmet when I left the apartment yesterday.

Yesterday. I was dead tired. Crashed on the futon, dozed off the moment I hit. Until I was woken by a loud, cracking noise. Thunder underground. Dishes dancing in the cupboards. The bathroom door sliding on its track, my suitcase wandering the apartment of its own will. The walls buckling and creaking. My body as heavy as iron. The floor lamp swaying. I reached out, tried to grab it before it fell on me. It crashed on the floor. The bulb exploding. Shards of glass everywhere. My head buried under the pillow. Hands clutching the futon for dear life. A painful sound tore through the building's bones. Then everything went silent again, motionless, little by little. I unclenched my fists. Withdrew my head from under my pillow. Dressed in a hurry. Grabbed my helmet and the rations box next to the door. And left without my phone or wallet or keys. I fled down the emergency stairs, heading to the street. All fifteen floors. A large man rode past me on a bike, grocery bags hanging from the handle bars. Another man and a woman were crossing the intersection. Hand in hand. Their shadows floated gently over the pavement, which was lit by a long line of street lamps, all set straight in the asphalt. No sirens. No fires. No debris. For two minutes I waited for the aftershocks, none came.

I was locked out.

Now. I spread the rations out between my legs. Four energy bars. Sugar cubes. Tea. A lighter. 500 millilitres of water. I bite into a bar. It's hard and dry. I chug all the water to make it easier to swallow the first bite, but if I plan to eat the rest of this without choking I'm going to need more, so I cup my hands and hold them out in the rain but I never saw the woman coming. My fingers skim her thighs. She jumps back. I spit the half-chewed energy bar into the palm of my left hand.

"Oh sorry, so sorry."

She ignores me. One of her hands awkwardly reaches into the bag hanging from her shoulder while the other shakes an imposing black umbrella.

"Oh you live here?"

She says 'yes' quietly without really looking in my direction.

"You're a lifesaver, I forgot my keys inside, would you be so kind as to let me in, please?"

"What floor do you live on?"

"On the fifteenth."

"I live on the fifteenth too and I've never seen you."

"That's because I just arrived yesterday... but I used to live here, before, with Arai Suzuko, maybe you've heard of her..."

"Oh... Sorry, I only moved in two months ago."

"She was famous. Suzuko, I mean."

But the lady pretends she didn't hear me, simply pushes the key into the lock.

"I left in a hurry yesterday, because of the earthquake..."

"Earthquake? I didn't feel anything."

"I guess it didn't cause any damage, except for the crazy mess in my apartment."

She squints hard at me.

"Your Japanese is really good."

"Thank you."

She opens the door.

"But I can't let you in."

"Ah, thank you."

I slip inside.

"I said I *can't* let you in."

"Oh sorry, I misunderstood."

27

"No you didn't, you understood me quite well!"

She stands in my way. I keep smiling.

"Oh I'd be eternally grateful to you if you'd let me at least sleep in the lobby."

This unsettles her.

"There are security cameras, you know."

"I live here, I swear. The doorman knows me. I was hoping to make it here before 10... He would have opened the door for me."

She casts a glance at her watch.

"It's 9:45."

"Oh he must be..."

But she doesn't look at me and she's not listening anymore either. I seize the opportunity, toss the lump of energy bar I had spat out a moment ago into the trash. And I spot the guard sleeping, sunken into a computer chair, legs crossed in front of a TV screen. I knock on his window. Grey eyes open and he hobbles out of his office, his back hunched, a cane in his hand which he shakily points at the lady, looking annoyed. He obviously heard parts of our conversation, tells her that he knows me and that I do, in fact, live on the fifteenth floor. She utters a few apologies, stabs the elevator button a dozen times hoping to bring it down faster. In vain. Eyes fixed on the floor. Mortally embarrassed.

"It's nothing, I'm the one who left my keys inside, it's my fault."

"No, no, I beg your pardon, I should have believed you."

"You don't have to apologize at all."

She's almost crying. Her face drooping. The old doorman scolding her like she's a kid.

"No, no, it's all my fault."

With every apology, though, I add more fuel to the doorman's fire. The lady, shoulders sagging now, hands on her knees, awaiting the beheading.

The elevator doors open finally. She rushes in. Relief. But only for a moment: the doorman orders her to wait for us.

There's not much air in the elevator. I'm soaked. Clothes heavy. Cold lungs. A puddle beneath my shoes. The lady shrinks into her corner. Umbrella closed. Her head facing the wall. I'm searching for something to say but nothing comes to mind. The doorman keeps his mouth shut too. Fondles his key ring. Calloused hands. Cracked fingernails. The elevator rising extraordinarily slowly.

Fifteenth floor.

Finally.

The guard gets out. I usher the woman ahead as I hold the door open for her. She avoids eye contact, shuffles off towards her apartment. The guard inserts a key into my lock. The lady inserts a key in hers, three doors down.

"There you go, it's open, do you need anything else?"

"No, thank you very much."

"It's nothing... and sorry about that lady. No class."

"No, no, I swear it was all my fault."

"Oh women are like..."

I don't give him a chance to finish the sentence. I lock the door behind me, take off my shoes, and walk through the apartment, abandoning my wet clothes on the floor wherever there's space. And it's weird. My suitcase is standing upright, on its wheels, at the end of the futon. The table hasn't moved. Or the dishes in the cupboard. And not a single shard of glass on the floor. But I watched the bulb from the floor lamp smash into a thousand little pieces yesterday. And I didn't clean up or put anything away before leaving. Strange. It hadn't all been a dream. Yet the apartment is in perfect order, as if there had never been an earthquake.

Three days later I make my way to Ono Gallery for the gathering Ayumi invited me to. I have nothing prepared. A few anecdotes in mind, that's it. But the gallery is packed. The men in pressed shirts. Relaxed, but not too much. The women in skirts or in dresses. Shoes, Adidas or Onitsuka Tiger. Cans of Yebisu in their hands. Polite conversation. I don't feel right. Ayumi said she wouldn't invite anyone I didn't know but I know almost no one here. Huge urge to turn tail and run. If I'd known there would be so many people here I'd have prepared differently. I would have written something down at least. Ayumi clears a path through the crowd, heading in my direction. Lips carmine red.

"So happy to see you, and I love this burnt orange colour (she pinches the sleeve of my shirt between her index finger and her thumb). The fabric is nice too, soft."

"Oh, Suzuko gave me this shirt, it's my favourite."

"I see."

"Hey Ayumi, where did all these people come from? You wrote the gathering would be small and informal."

"Oh but the event *is* informal, just look at me."

She runs her hands down both sides of her hips like in a 1980s clothing commercial. Black dress, simple and short, perfectly tailored. Cobalt tights.

"Uhh... I don't really see what's so informal about what you're wearing. It's perfect."

"And what about these old runners?"

She raises her heels and twists her feet one after the other. Her Adidas are barely scuffed.

"Uhh..."

"Alright, I kind of got carried away with the invitations, I admit."

She laughs.

"I'm sorry but Suzuko attracts a crowd, it isn't my fault. Everyone loved her."

"Oh Ayumi, please don't talk about Suzuko in the past tense. It breaks my heart."

She looks sheepish for a moment, then forces herself to smile at me. Lips forming a terrible frown.

"Come, everyone's dying to hear you. Don't worry, you're going to be great."

She slides her hand down the length of my arm to the bend in my elbow. Suddenly my eyes water over.

"I'm here, Vincent, don't be scared."

I sigh.

"Oh we can cancel if you prefer, no problem."

"No, I want to talk about Suzuko. I... She was so... I..."

"Oh, you're right, talking about her in the past tense is awful. I'm sorry."

"No, no, it's my fault."

"No it's me, sorry."

I tilt my head forward a bit.

"Alright, Ayumi... That'll do, enough apologizing. We'll start when you want."

The back of the gallery, standing. Maybe forty people facing me, on chairs arranged in rows. Ayumi introduces me with great affection. I'm moved. I open my mouth but nothing comes out. Not right away anyways.

People begin trickling out of the gallery. Some thank me politely for my talk but I fear I've disappointed everyone. I head towards the exit. Ayumi accompanies me. We stop in the door frame, stand next to each other.

"I'm exhausted."

"Don't worry, Vincent, it was really good."

"Thanks but that's not it. I... It's not easy..."

"I know, everyone could tell, don't worry. You speak about Suzuko with such... with such tenderness."

"I spent most of the time looking for the right words to say."

"It was perfect."

"But it went nowhere. And I drank four or five beers too fast. The ones your assistant served me. I don't feel good."

I step outside.

"Wait Vincent, would you happen to be free Saturday?"

"Uhh... I think so..."

"I might have a proposition for you..."

"Oh yeah? What is it?"

"Could you come to the gallery at two on Saturday? I'll tell you then. I'd like to..."

But someone grabs me from behind before she can finish her sentence. I turn around. A big man, communist beard, nose ring like a bull's.

"Hey! Pavle!"

"No way, Vincent, what are you doing here? Why didn't you tell me you were back in town?"

"I got back less than a week ago... but I was thinking about you."

He grabs me in a bear hug. It breathes new life in me for a moment.

"Ayumi, do you know Pavle Jovovic?"

"Oh Suzuko used to talk about him, but we've never officially been introduced."

"Pleased to meet you."

"Delighted."

They bow towards each other. Pavle, all smiles, pats me on the shoulder a few times.

"Alright, I'm going to let you two catch up, ok? I've got some work to do."

"Until next time."

She leaves.

"Pavle, you have no idea how much I missed Tokyo."

"I never leave the city, so I don't actually know what that's like. How long are you staying this time?"

"I don't know, for the moment I've only got a three-month visa."

"Where're you living?"

"Still in Sumida, you?"

"Oh, I needed a change. Minori and I just bought a little studio in Ueno."

"Awesome! You guys billionaires now?"

"Haha, not really. For the moment there's just about a roof and a floor, we ripped everything out."

"You doing renos together, you and Minori?"

"Yeah."

"I can't wait to see it, it'll be magnificent, I have no doubt."

"I hope so, for the moment though it's more Sarajevo 1995!"

"Right up your alley."

"You know me."

"That I do."

"What brings you back to Tokyo?"

"Well... to be honest..."

Pavle takes a step back.

"Wait Vincent, you're still in Sumida?"

"Yeah, like I just said."

"Don't tell me..."

"Don't tell you what?"

"Tell me that's not what you're doing!"

"Uhh... what's that?"

"No... you didn't really move back into that place you shared with Suzuko, did you?"

He places two big hands on my shoulders. They're heavy.

"Fuck! That's unhealthy!"

"Well... I couldn't find anything else."

"Hold it! There are like a million apartments in Tokyo!"

"Yeah but I know the doorman, and you know what it's like trying to find a decent place in a nice location, especially as a foreigner."

"But you speak perfect Japanese."

"Ennh, not as good as you think."

He rolls his eyes.

"It's alright, Pavle, it's a nice apartment."

"Who cares if it's nice? That's not the issue."

He pulls me behind one of the steel supports framing the entry to the gallery.

"Listen, I know a lot of people in Tokyo, I'm sure I can find you an apartment."

"Thanks but that won't be necessary."

"It'd be much better."

"I'm perfectly fine where I am."

He shakes his head, annoyed.

"Nah."

"No what?"

"There's no way you can be perfectly fine."

"Bah..."

"Why don't you move to Ueno? It'll be cool. Everyone's moving there nowadays."

I lean a shoulder against the gallery's glass façade. On the other side one of Ayumi's assistants is measuring the space between two walls with a measuring tape. Silently I watch her work for about a minute.

"Anyway... What brings you back to Tokyo, other than the urge to reopen old wounds?"

"I'm not reopening old wounds."

"Oh yeah? Why did you come back?"

"It's not easy..."

"Huh, living in the same apartment..."

"Would you just drop it!"

"Ok."

Pavle backs down.

"How are you, otherwise?"

"Oh I don't know. I think about her all the time. On my way home the other night I could've sworn I saw her on the street."

"Oh... I'm sure that's normal."

"It's like she's still here. Everywhere. I can feel her."

"I feel her too, sometimes, a little. She was my friend."

"I know."

He wraps his arms around me.

"I'm always here, if you need me. Really."

"Thanks Pavle."

"We'll have to go get drunk soon!"

"Gladly. And then you can show me Sarajevo 1995."

"Ah of course!"

Pavle Jovovic is a painter, Serbian originally. One of the few foreigners to naturalize as a Japanese citizen. He designs huge pieces of art, sections of walls where he blends the motifs tradition-ally found in Serbian and Croatian tapestries. Of course, at first glance I never know which motifs are Serbian and which are Croatian. That's kind of the whole thing: we wage war thinking we're radically different. And then no.

On February 3, 1995, when he was 18 years old, he came to Tokyo as a refugee. His mother and father, his little sister, his grand-parents, cousins, friends and neighbours. All dead. In the street or at home, in their cars, in the kitchen or in their bedrooms, in the fields, in the office, in combat. Bombs, always bombs.

The following Saturday at 2 p.m. I'm standing in front of Ono Gallery, as planned. But the door's locked. Inside a young man is drilling a hole in a wall, lying face down on the concrete. I knock. The young man looks up, drops his tools and comes to open the door for me. His face is familiar. Most likely one of Ayumi's assistants.

"Sorry to bother you but I have an appointment with Ayumi at two o'clock..."

He squints.

"I'm sorry but I don't speak Japanese," he says in English.

"Oh I thought you were Ayumi's assistant, sorry. I'm Vincent."

"Li Yi-Fan."

"Oh! I saw your exhibition here two years ago!"

Subconsciously he begins massaging his left hand.

"Oh yeah... That exhibit..."

"I'm glad you survived!"

"Haha, yes, I'm glad too. I lost quite a bit of blood that night."

Then, suddenly, Ayumi is there, on the other side of the room, appearing seemingly from nowhere. We watch her, Li Yi-Fan and me, as she crosses the room towards us. Light. Smiling. Affectionately she lays both hands on Li Yi-Fan's shoulders. Then asks him "how's the installation going?" with an impeccable British accent.

"Very well, thanks."

"Fantastic. Vincent and I are going out for lunch, but my assistants will be staying in, so if you need anything, please do not hesitate to ask them. Or you can of course call me if you prefer."

"No worries Ayumi, I'll be fine."

She releases his shoulders and hooks her arm around my elbow before leading me to the exit. I've never known a Japanese woman to be so touchy-feely.

Shōwa Avenue.
Lunchtime crowds.

"Do you remember Li Yi-Fan's last exhibit?"

"I mostly remember he left in an ambulance."

"Oh yeah, what a disaster, that's all they talked about in the press. Luckily your article was there to save the day."

"My article? I'd be surprised if more than three people read it."

"Oh don't exaggerate. There are at least four people on the editing team at *Initiales*..."

"Haha, true!"

"I'm happy to exhibit his work again. Will you come to the vernissage? It's next week."

"Of course I'll be there! That'll take me back a bit, that night was the first time I went to Suzuko's workshop."

"It's also the first time we met, you and I."

She's holding me as we walk down the street. Is she flirting with me? I run into someone on the sidewalk.

"Oh pardon me."

We turn left down a narrow, busy pedestrian street.

"Here it is."

She lets go of my arm.

"What's here?"

"Singaporean specialties. Just opened. Organic. Delicious. I've ridden the subway for over an hour a few times these past few weeks just to come here."

"Like a pregnant woman."

"Hahaha yes but no."

We go in.

An aroma of caramel and spice.

Ayumi buys us both a few bakkwa, Chinese jerky. It's all the kiosk sells. No table or counter to eat at. Just a cramped, crowded hallway. But they just finished building a terrace on the roof. We take the elevator.

Eighteenth floor.

A few pots and planters. Tables and stools. And a raised platform of sorts where we grab a seat. To our left a woman, alone, a cup in hand. Shoulder length hair, perfectly straight bangs. Another woman a little farther, alone too, staring at her phone. Sunglasses. Crows. Wind and dust.

"For the moment, very few people know about this terrace. The building isn't tall enough for an unimpeded view but we take what we can get. It'll be hopping up here come June."

"Your secret's safe with me, don't you worry about that."

"You can tell your friends, of course."

"Ok... and if I ever publish anything—I could set a scene here, starring us—I'd make damn sure the place isn't easy to find."

"Oh, are you saying... Are you working on a book?"

"I'm still not quite sure where it's headed, but yes."

"What's it about?"

"Hmmmm... Something more realistic than what I usually write, I think, more personal, more... emotionally... hard to write. Anyway, you didn't take me out to lunch just so we can talk about my stories. What did you want to ask me?"

She places both her hands on her knees.

"It's a little hard to ask you but..."

"I'm listening, Ayumi."

"Are you the one who has Suzuko's head?"

"Her last head, you mean? Yes, I have it. Why?"

"Well it's... I'd like to organize a retrospective."

"Hmmm..."

"You don't have to worry, I'd only borrow it for as long as the exhibit's up. I've already contacted a few collectors, most of them have offered to lend any pieces of Suzuko's art they might have to the gallery."

"I... isn't there enough material at her workshop?"

There's no answer. She lowers her eyes.

"What?"

Her hands lightly clench her tights.

"What is it, Ayumi?"

"It's just, the workshop's been emptied out."

"Oh..."

"Sorry, I thought you knew..."

"Oh, ah, no, but I should have guessed... I've been gone three months."

"All her things are safe, don't worry. I have a storage locker in Itabashi. It's a little ways out but..."

"I see... So that's all you need then, her head?"

"What do you mean?"

"Well is that all you wanted to ask me?"

"Not quite all... Actually... What I'd like... is for you to work with me on the exhibit, for us to set it up together. The two of you had such a unique bond."

I sigh. A crow bounces on the guardrail.

"How long are you planning to stay in Tokyo this time?"

"As long as possible. But to get a long term visa I need to have a job... Something official. Teaching English in a school, for example."

"Oh, but you hated teaching English!"

"No I didn't... Well... Not as much as you think. Anyway, I don't really have much of a choice if I want to stay."

"If you agree to work with me on Suzuko's exhibition I'll write you a letter of employment which you can use to get a two-year working visa."

I remove a bakkwa from its paper wrapper.

"A retrospective on Suzuko? Already? Isn't it a little soon?"

"If we want the exhibit to happen sometime within the next two years, the work has to start sooner rather than later."

I don't know what to say. And Ayumi knows it.

"Take some time to think about it. It's not easy, I know..."

A crow lands loudly on the stool to our left. I pinch the bakkwa between my fingers but I don't bring it to my mouth. Ayumi places a hand on my arm.

"Oh Vincent, I didn't want to... Forgive me."

I walk along Shōwa-dori towards the east, tossing around in my mind the proposal Ayumi just made me. I pass under the elevated highway. I turn right. The weather is beautiful, cool and dry. I breathe in deeply. The streets are wide. The skyscrapers, light. Empty streets, crowded streets. Until Sumida. My neighbourhood. Tamer than Ginza, of course. I take the left and walk around Morishita station. And I see her. Suzuko. Crossing the intersection towards the main street. It's the route we used to take together whenever we left the neighbourhood. Every time.

She keeps walking, a hop in her step. The curve of her shoulders. The red in her scarf.

I could have easily caught up to her on my bike. I wish I had taken it with me to go meet Ayumi. Suzuko turns right and disappears, just past the hair salon on the corner. I turn right, in pursuit, on to Shin-Ōhashi. There she is. Fifty metres ahead of me. She's hurrying along in a straight line, passing all the other pedestrians.

I'm walking fast, or rather, I'm running. The distance between us narrows.

Suzuko is at the bridge now. It's half a kilometre long at least. I'm going to catch up to her, that much is for sure. I think for a moment. I feel light. Terribly light. I slow down somewhat. The air is fresher closer to the water. There's no need to rush. When we're halfway across the bridge I'll grab her by the waist. She'll jump. It'll be funny. I hope. I comb my hair with my fingers. I straighten my jacket. Good enough. I'm presentable. But Suzuko doesn't step onto the bridge. She turns left onto the path skirting the river and disappears behind an apartment tower. It's alright, I'll still catch up to her. She's only about twenty metres ahead of me. But when I get to the corner there's no one in sight. Above, blue sky. Below, grey asphalt. Even lower, the black water of the river.

"Suzuko!"

My voice falls flat amidst the towering buildings and the side of the bridge.

I feel ridiculous.

I wander around the neighbourhood for an hour. The takoyaki stand we passed a thousand times. The smell of fried dough. Coconut oil. Squid. The silkscreen shop that doubles as a brewery. She's the one who showed me the place. Bare trees. The erotic video store we'd sometimes go into for a little laugh. The ten-storey pachinko. The streets without sidewalks around our place. The canal. Where we would often stroll in the evenings.

I walk along beside it. Cyclists and joggers. The square next to our building. Reserves of water and food under the benches, in case of earthquakes. A cat crosses the street. Suzuko would have stopped to pet it. I walk on by. I turn the key in the lock on the ground floor. The sound of the mechanism. The weight of the door. Suzuko's distinct smell in the entryway. In the elevator. In the apartment. A smell of fur and saliva, of leather and glue, of dust and sugar.

January 20. 9:30 p.m. Ueno. A popular bar. Patina wood counters. Stone floors. Unexpected marquetry ceilings. Metallic ventilation tubes. Pavle's waiting for me on a stool facing the imposing wall-to-ceiling window. We hug warmly.

"So happy to see you."

"Me too!"

"I already ordered saké. That ok?"

"Perfect. I'll get the next round. Kampai!"

"Hey I managed to find you a place!"

"Oh Pavle don't start with that!"

"What? It's a great place, not far from here. An architect friend is going to be working in Rome from February to June."

Outside it's starting to snow. Big, lazy flakes. White like the fur of a hare.

"He was just about to hire a company to come water his plants and dust the apartment while he's away, can you believe that? He'll rent it to you cheap. That'll give you time to find a job. And you'd be alone to write. It's big, you'll see."

People on the other side of the vast window are taking pictures of the falling snow, the night lights. Reflections in azure and rose and lime.

"So what do you think?"

"Well... I'd prefer to stay in Sumida for the moment, it suits me fine. And besides, I have a writing routine in that apartment. Also, I love the view, it's inspiring, I'm attached to that place, you know?"

"Bah, not really, no."

I drink the rest of my saké and serve myself some more.

"I mean, yes, obviously, I can understand that you want to stay in the apartment where you and Suzuko lived together. But at the same time I think you'd be better off somewhere else. Her presence is embedded in the walls, and in the sheets, in everything. I've said it once and I'll say it again, it's not healthy."

"Hmmm..."

"You still hallucinating, seeing her everywhere?"

"I'm not so sure they were hallucinations..."

He empties his glass in one swig and serves us both some more, disappointment on his face.

"Bah, fine, but you should really consider my friend's place, it's an interesting space. The view is nice too. You should check it out before making up your mind, don't you think?"

I don't answer. I empty my glass.

"No one else is going to take it if you don't. Besides, the opportunity was too good to pass up, I already told my friend you'd take care of his plants. Now I'm going to have to tell him that it just isn't going to work... I hate cancelling at the last minute."

"Well, to be fair, that's your problem. I never said I wanted to move."

"I know but you'd be crazy not to."

He rolls up his shirt sleeves. Forearms splattered with paint.

"You're the one who wants me to move, not me. I don't understand..."

"Hold on a sec, are you blaming me for wanting what's good for you?"

"What's good? I've told you a dozen times at least that I don't want to move. Maybe sometime in the future but right now, no. I'm not ready."

"Well, Ayumi also thinks you..."

"Stop pushing this, Pavle! I don't give a shit what Ayumi thinks."

"Fuck Vincent, look, you're not doing so hot, I can see that. You got some terrible bags under your eyes."

"It's the jetlag."

"Jetlag... It's been two weeks since you got back! No, you're... I don't know..."

He fills our cups with saké.

"Look, I just want to help you out a little. Seeing Suzuko in the streets, that's not normal. And you're feeling earthquakes where there are none."

"I'm sensitive to earthquakes, always have been, I feel them even when they're small."

"Imperceptible, you mean."

"That's not the point."

He breathes in deeply. We drain our cups in silence, both of us facing the street. People passing by. Snow barely sticking to the ground.

"Should I order something else?"

He shakes his head.

"You'd be much better off in Ueno..."

"Fuck, Pavle, enough! I could care less what you think! Did you even bother thinking of asking me what I thought? Who exactly is it you're trying to help? I don't fucking care that your friend's going to Rome! I don't give a shit if his apartment is great! I won't move just because it'd help him with his plants. For fuck's sake!"

I slam my glass on the counter.

Pavle unrolls his shirt sleeves, slowly, grabs his jacket and storms off.

I stay. Shaking. My hands clenched. Things aren't going well, not at all. I breathe out. It's hard to breathe. Pavle crosses the road. Toque pulled tight over his head. I tilt the glass of saké back into my mouth but there's only a drop left.

Fuck. Suzuko, walking by on the sidewalk.

There. Right outside the tall windows. The way she moves, that's her alright. Wool gloves on her hands. Her hips, her shoulders. So fine. I could dash for the exit, chase after her, catch her. But I stay inside. I mutter, willing her to hear me, "come on, turn your head, Suzuko, turn your head, now, look, I'm here, look, turn your head." But she keeps walking, straight ahead, as though I didn't exist.

I hop on my bike but I don't head for home.
I need to ride. Southwards, randomly, then east
along the Kanda River. My wheel tracks in the
thin layer of snow. Moored barges. All white.
City noises partially absorbed. 0°C. Mittens.
Headband. Wind breaker. Akihabara. We would
stroll here from time to time, Suzuko and I. On
winter nights like this one. For the fun of it. It's
crowded. Young people and old people. Stores
open after midnight. Teens dressed up as school-
girls trying to lure drunks into shady basements.
Buildings like radioactive tubes. Snow. A nuclear
winter. The Fukushima catastrophe not even ten
years ago. It suddenly comes to mind. I was living
in Osaka then. Some of my colleagues in those
days wanted to emigrate to Europe or America
but time passed, they stayed in Japan. Osaka is
far from Fukushima and was barely affected by
the disaster. Tokyo, on the other hand, is still

57

recording abnormally high levels of radioactivity in 2018.

The snow has become little flurries now, biting.

I wander the neighbourhood, zigzagging from one street to another. Deep down I don't want to go back to the apartment. Pavle was right. It would probably be best if I moved out. But I don't know. It's not easy. Without realizing it I pass the same place ten times in a row. Dazzling lights, blinding. Women in phosphorescent kimonos, candy pink eyelids, glitter on their cheeks. Akihabara. Neighbourhood for insomniacs. Suzuko sometimes came here to recharge. Slowly I ride down the street, along the sidewalks. I watch, I look, I examine, can't help myself. Suzuko, now would be a good time to show yourself on one of these street corners, I tell myself. But there's nothing but hollow forms. Cutouts of her body appearing at times in the light. Dark shapes. A void. Impressions of what's missing. The presence of absence.

Finally I head home. Cross through the lobby. Take the elevator. Fifteenth floor. My apartment. I pull the door open. A draft of icy air. I turn the lights on, take my shoes off. Almost as cold inside as it is outside. Snow has blown in through an open window, I go close it. A trail of clear water leading to the futon, pooling up underneath. I swear I had closed everything before I left, though. My head's elsewhere. That's what I tell myself as I wipe the floor with a dishrag. I wring it out over the kitchen sink. I go to bed. Exhausted.

The next few days I'm on my bike. Riding around. Neighbourhood after neighbourhood. Bike paths. Along the canals. The cemeteries of Aoyama and Yanaka. Dark trees and dead grass. Every route we ever took together. Suzuko and I.

Every night I sit at the kitchen table. Facing the glass wall. Outside, the city. The Skytree. Ryōgoku Stadium. Winter skies. The Sumida River, cold and dark.

My computer on the table. My fingers resting on the keyboard like on the keys of a synthesizer. Everything I write writes itself. Quiet night beyond the glass wall. More than sixty pages since I got back to Tokyo.

This book I write with her.

Without her.

I feel lost, alone, distraught. Tons of images in my mind. Intermittent. Sentences, one, then another. Syncopated. Her name often. Her name everywhere. In every word. In every landscape. In the depth of the screen. In the thickness of the pages.

Suzuko.

It's late. The elevated metro line has stopped crossing the river. Ad space for popsicles made from peas. The black and orange illuminated stripes of an overpass. A green trellis fence abandoned on the roof of the building opposite. My grey Muji notebook on the table to the left of my computer. The yellow scarf Suzuko gave me. An empty bowl. The permanent impression of her lips on the edges of the china. Her silhouette on the balcony. The shape of her body under the blanket.

Good evening Vincent

                    Hi

I'm not bothering you? What are
you doing?

                    Writing stuff, I'm at home.

I just spoke with Pavle.

                    Ah. What did he have to
                    say?

He's lived in Japan for some
twenty years now, but he isn't
quite as delicate as us Japanese
yet. He might not know how to say
it properly, but he's worried about
you.

You know, not every
Japanese person is delicate,
Ayumi.

Of course not.

Pavle didn't mean to hurt
me, I know. And I know that
I should move, one day, that
it'd be good for me, in a way.
But the conversation I had
with Pavle made me want to
stay. To spite him a bit. It's
dumb.

It's true that moving wouldn't
be such a bad thing for you. But
I understand, it's hard.

To find an apartment in
Tokyo? That's for sure.

Stop it
That's not it

I know
I miss her
So much
I don't know what to do
anymore

Oh why don't you stop by the
gallery, we'll go grab a drink.

> That's nice of you but I don't
> really feel like going out.
> And, I've been meaning to
> tell you, about the exhibit
> for Suzuko, and working on
> it together, I think it'd be
> best if I told you no right
> now.

Don't worry about it. I thought it
could be good for you.
What did you do with the notes
you took last year?

> They're on my computer.
> I'll send them to you if you
> want, but they're not in
> Japanese, you know.

Ok. I'll ask you, if I need them.
(*'⌣')
Did you find a teaching job?

> No but to tell you the truth
> I really don't want to do
> that.

What are you going to do to get a
visa then?

>   I don't know. I might just go
>   back to Montreal and live
>   there.

What!? But you said you wanted
to stay in Tokyo!

>   You and Pavle are right,
>   I should move.

No wait! We never meant that you
should leave Japan!

>   What's keeping me here?

Suzuko's ghost

>   Haha
>   All the more reason to go
>   back to Montreal!

Look, I'm not saying this to
pressure you, but I'll hire you on a
contract. That way you'll be able to
get a two-year visa.

No obligation to work for any
exhibition.
Just a contract, that's it.

I'll think about it

Think about it later. The contract
will be ready in a week.
Just a piece of paper. No
obligation, I swear!
At least you'd be able to stay in
Tokyo.

You're a lifesaver

It's nothing

It's not nothing. Thank you
<3

No need to thank me

Ok fine. I'm not thanking
you then.

Haha
Are you coming to Li Yi-Fan's
vernissage tomorrow?

                No

Come! It'll do you good! A lot of
people you know are going to be
there!

                Hmmm. Ok. Maybe.
                But I should let you go.
                I'd like to finish the chapter
                I'm working on tonight.

Oh for the book you were telling
me about?

                Maybe
                I hope so
                Yes

February 1. Ono Gallery. Packed. DJ in the corner, discreet. Pavle at the bar. He's two heads taller than everyone else. I linger alongside a wall. Don't really feel like going to talk to him for the moment. I take the can of Yebisu from one of Ayumi's assistants. Ayumi. She's chatting with Li Yi-Fan in the middle of the gallery. I wave at her when our eyes meet. She smiles at me. I say hi to two or three acquaintances here and there but I don't get dragged into a conversation. Don't really feel like being here. Suzuko on my mind. Maybe I should have stayed home.

This is the second exhibition for Li Yi-Fan that Ayumi's organized. The last one was about two years ago. And at first glance the concept is the same. Li Yi-Fan cut some twenty holes in various walls around the gallery. To slip your head in the highest ones you have to stand on a narrow step ladder, to slip your head in the

69

lowest you have to crawl or lay flat on the floor. I stop in front of a hole placed at shoulder height. First I read what's written on the piece of cardboard glued to the right of the piece (an orgy scene, artfully described). Then I stick my head into the hole. Where everything is dark. I wait for a projection to start. I keep waiting. Until I start to make out the bodies piled on top of each other in the darkness. Moaning in my ears. But it might just be the muffled echo of the noise in the gallery. Or just my imagination running wild after what I just read on the cardboard.

I take my head out of the hole.

To my left a woman is lying face down on the floor, her head inserted in the only hole cut at that level. I admire her courage. She's wearing a snow white hoodie which will undoubtedly no longer be white once she gets back up. Her back forms a narrow valley, the tips of her shoulder blades pointy mountains. A winter landscape. Her calves nonchalantly swaying in the air. Long legs. Fitted grey chinos, capris. Black socks. Turquoise and burnt yellow Pumas. Her outfit is so well put together she almost looks like an anime character. I, on the other hand, have a big nose. That's what they always tell me. It took me a while to understand that in

Japan "you have a big nose" is a compliment. There's nothing excessive about the size of my nose though. I think about that for a moment. It's been a few minutes now that the woman's head has been in the hole. I'm intrigued. I press my hand against the wall while I await my turn. The conversation in the room is polite. There's drinking. There's some laughing, but not too much. She takes her head out of the hole, turns around, and sits flat against the wall. And my heart skips when I see her face. Her eyelids, to be precise. They're thick, bright red, a glossy vermilion line surrounding them, as if the edges had been cut with a scalpel. I'm mesmerized but I manage to find my voice.

"Sorry, are you done? Can I look in your hole?"

"It's not my hole."

No time for blushing. She waves her hand, motioning for me to join her on the floor. I lie face down. Cool concrete. I stick my head into the opening.

I stay there for a minute, then sit back against the wall next to the woman.

"Did you like it?"

"Yes. Hmmm... It reminds me of *Tokyo Story*, the film by Ozu. There's a scene where two characters go up the Tokyo Tower to look out over the city. Ozu only films their faces, never what they see. It's weird. Usually viewers get to see what the characters are looking at. Shot, reverse shot. Ozu refuses to give it up. And that's what makes the scene so powerful. Because it's been amputated, cut in half."

"The absence, then?"

"Yes. Did you like it?"

"A lot."

"Why?"

She rubs her sweater.

"Because I got my pure white hoodie dirty."

"Haha."

"All these people so nicely dressed... I bet no one other than us two will dare to lie on the ground in front of the rest of the cool crowd. And, from this angle, it's kind of nice. Look at all those legs... like a forest."

"With a canopy of little panties."

"Haha, yeah, and look at him, he's got Pokémon socks!"

"Oh how cute."

We laugh.

She takes a few pictures.

All those legs. Grey. Black. Blue. Bare. Shadows and light. Fabric and skin. Spilled beer. Sticky little puddles. A show I could watch for hours. The woman is staring at the crowd too. A long pair of shoes cross the room. Pavle's. I might go speak with him in a bit, apologize for getting annoyed the other night. I see Ayumi's legs. Bare. They come closer. Stop one metre in front of us.

"I'm happy to see you enjoying this exhibit like no one else, Vincent."

I look up.

"Oh yes, everything's great, seen from down here, I love it."

"We're going to go eat after the vernissage, with the group. You coming with?"

"Sure."

I'd be happy just sitting here on the ground but she holds out a hand to help me up. Then leads me through the crowd until one of her assistants comes to whisper something in her ear. She sighs as she rolls her eyes.

"I have to go fix a little problem..."

"Ah ok."

"I'll see you in a bit."

"Perfect."

I turn around. The woman is behind me. Standing. Eyelids like over-ripened cherries.

"Sorry, we weren't introduced. I'm Vincent."

"Pleased to meet you. I'm..."

She hesitates. She looks to the right, to the left, as if looking for something.

"I– I'm Kana."

After the vernissage we head to a Chinese restaurant behind Takarachō station. Noisy. Dark.
A cloud of cigarette smoke. A long rectangular table. Twenty people around it. Pavle and
I huddled together in the curve of a booth. Kana
sitting at the other end of the table. An impres-
sive buffet between the two of them. Juicy balls
of all kinds. Ruby and emerald. Pancakes and
doughnuts that smell like honey, and spices,
and herbs, and the ocean. Green and yellow and
red vegetables. Roots and crustaceans. There's
even a bowl full of white, plump larva which
is apparently super popular in China. I didn't
know you could find it in Japan. I grab one with
my chopsticks and bring it to my lips. Onto my
tongue. I roll it around. Fleshy. But the thing
breaks apart easily. Like a soft-boiled egg. The
yolk runny, creamy, slightly sour. Kana also puts
a larva in her mouth. Sucks it in. Eyelids closed,

blood-red, puffy. Cheeks sunken in as if sucking on a lemon. She devours three more before leaning in over the table, chopsticks pointed, grabbing everything she can, stuffing her mouth like a starving child. Her neighbours chat among themselves, avoid talking to her. At least, that's the impression I'm getting. Maybe I shouldn't have invited her.

Pavle grabs me by the shoulders.

"How are you, Vincent?"

"Alright."

He hugs me warmly for a moment, as if we had never fought. All animosity dissipated in a single embrace. We clink our glasses, holding them in front of us.

"My friend finally found someone to take care of his place while he's gone, no need to worry."

"Oh it's all forgotten, no problem."

He fills our glasses. I empty mine in two swigs.

"Say, Pavle, you see that woman at the other end of the table?"

"Which one?"

"The one wolfing everything down, there. I just met her tonight... Do you know her?"

"Uhh... (he isn't quite looking in Kana's direction) why are you asking me?"

"No reason, just because."

76

Pavle refills my cup right to the brim. I sip up the excess before drinking the rest in one gulp. Baijiu. Great stuff!

"It's weird, Pavle, I have to tell ya..."

"What?"

"After we met the other night... I saw Suzuko walk by out front of the bar."

"Ah."

"I've seen her so many times since I got back to Tokyo."

"Yeah, you told me the other day."

For a few long moments he says nothing, looking stricken. He lowers his head gloomily, his hands on the table. I grab a baby calamari with my fingers. Toss it in my mouth. I love these. He picks up his glass in his fist, knocks back his drink with one swig and fills both our cups again. I'm staring off into space. He plants his black chopsticks in his bowl of white rice. Sticks of funeral incense. His way of saying that he's thinking of Suzuko, I know.

"Here Vincent, to forgetting!"

He lifts his glass and everyone around the table does so as well, spontaneously.

"Kampai! Kampai!! Kampai!!!"

The empty bottles are quickly replaced by full ones, like magic. Bodies unwind. Belts are loosened. The women go to the washroom and come back a hundred times more beautiful. The men crush their cigarette butts right into their bowls of rice, take their ties off, unbutton their shirts. Kana's eyelids shine in the smoky darkness. Two lanterns. It's getting hot in here. People trade places around the table.

Stolen glances between Kana and I.

The men around her bounce back to life.

Ayumi comes to join me in the booth. She's tipsy. I'm pretty tipsy myself. She wraps her arms around my head and pulls me down towards her neck. Kana shrinks into her chair as she stares at me. Her back suddenly slumping in despair. The white hoodie peppered with sauce, like a Jackson Pollock drip painting. And her eyelids. So puffy they half devour her. I only have eyes for her. I get up with the intention to go sit near Kana but Ayumi holds me back by my waist. It's nothing. Ayumi has always been more touchy-feely with westerners. It isn't me. At least I don't think so. I'm not thinking anymore. Too much alcohol. It's all good. But I want to go sit with Kana. In a ball in her chair, now. Kana. So happy a mere ten minutes ago. Ayumi fills my glass. I spill the whole thing down my neck. The one-too-many. There aren't twenty people around the table anymore but forty, fifty, sixty. My body, in the booth, wrecked. The pungent smell of the seat. The clinking of glasses. Clicking of utensils. The icky sounds of swallowing. The dry scraping of lighters. The sizzling of tobacco. Kana's fiery eyelids.

And.

Then nothing.

Hi Kana. Sorry about last
night, I asked you to come
to the restaurant and we
didn't even get to talk.
I could have at least said
goodnight! (x_x)

Oha Vincent. Don't be sorry, I'm
the one who left suddenly.

Oh yeah? I shouldn't have
had so much to drink. You
alright?

Yes, thank you. But I ate way too
much last night, I don't know what
got into me, I was starving. I didn't
feel so good afterwards.

It happens.

ヾ(๐^ω^๐)ノ

Would you be up for going
for a drink next week?

You free tomorrow afternoon?

Not sure I'll be over my
Baijiu hangover from
yesterday...

。：°(｡/ω＼｡)°・。

But at the same time I feel
much better already (o _O)

3pm, Ikejiri-Ōashi station? We
could go for a walk through
Meguro garden.

Oh I love that place!

°+｡:.°ヽ(*´∀`)ノ°.:。+°

Whoa! My kaomoji game
isn't quite up to par
＼(O...O)／

See you tomorrow! ヾ(･ω･*ʋ

Meguro Garden is at the top of a seven-storey concrete structure, lost among a jumble of highways, which are also six, seven, eight storeys up. We go up in an elevator. Beautiful afternoon. 5°C. Middle of winter. Dry. The snowy peak of Mount Fuji, in the distance between the skyscrapers. The crystal blue of the sky. Almost no one in the garden. Young cherry trees planted alongside the paths. Their thin branches dry and dark. No leaves or flowers. Crows.

Kana and I walk side by side and I can really feel her left hand swaying only a centimetre to my right. Our fingers sometimes brush against each other, naturally. I don't know if she feels it too.

"I heard about a group exhibit being organized by Gallery 3331... The vernissage is in three weeks, would you like to come with me, Kana?"

"I'd love to. A friend of mine actually has a piece at that show."

"Oh yeah? Who's your friend?"

"Pavle Jovovic," (then she hides her mouth behind her hands as if she shouldn't have spoken).

"Oh I know him! He didn't tell me he has a piece at 3331!"

"Eeeh... actually, I don't think I'm supposed to know that either. Forget what I just said, ok? I'm sure he wanted to keep it a secret... It's kind of the spirit of the show."

"Ah ok... I'll act cool. How do you know Pavle?"

She doesn't answer. We reach the end of the path. A thick wall of glass separates us from an interchange. Cars rush by in silence under the garden.

"I have to leave soon, Vincent. I... I have a meeting at 4:30."

"Ok, no worries."

Already 4.

We leave the garden by the steep stairwell that leads to the Meguro River, which we follow a hundred metres upstream, until Ikejiri-Ōhashi subway. We stand facing each other for a moment in front of the station. I want to ask her why her eyelids are so red. Red coral. Red flame. Thick and glistening. The astonishing red suits her so well, after all, you'd swear it was the most natural shade of eyelid in the world. She looks me straight in the eye. Maybe she's waiting for a compliment about her makeup... or for me to ask if her eyes are ok... But... I don't want to insult her by suggesting that her eyelids look unhealthy if they are just covered in makeup, but on the other hand, I don't want to go on about her makeup if her eyelids are swimming in infection. So I say nothing. I look. Her eyelids barely open. Voluptuous and inviting. I have a terrible urge to kiss them. But Kana disappears into the subway before I can try anything.

Hundreds of people exit the subway. Hundreds of people enter. At regular intervals. And I think I've spotted Suzuko at least ten times. Suzuko. I realize I hadn't thought of her even one second while I was walking with Kana. Kana. I like her, that's for sure. But still. Four and a half months is nothing. Four and a half months. Only. Barely. Since Suzuko died. September 15, 2017. So near yet so far. Yesterday like a second ago. Tomorrow like a thousand years from now. Elsewhere. Little by little. The anguish. Comes and goes. No obvious reason. Things could have gone differently. Things can always go differently. The lives we never live. If only I had. And Kana now. Kana. Wanting to let myself be carried away. For the moment. Nothing more. Nothing bad. Vibrating. Something's vibrating. Inside. My pocket. Oh my phone. Which brings me back to reality. The entrance to the subway. Hundreds of people rushing. Suzuko nowhere to be seen. I grab my phone. If it's Kana I'm going to write to her that I wanted to kiss her before she left. Maybe. To see. Just like that. Because you should always seize those moments when there is still nothing to lose.

Thanks for the walk, it was nice. I'm sorry I had to leave so quickly
J||o・-・)ﾉ

You don't have to apologize. It was perfect. Meguro garden is my favourite place in the world!

Mine too!

I hope your meeting won't be too bad. It's so nice out. And it's Saturday! By the way... what is this meeting?

Oh this is my stop, I have to get off. Talk to you soon!
ヽ(=・ω・=)ﾉ

Wait. I wanted to tell you that... Well, I wanted to kiss

you in front of the subway
just now. Would you have
let me?

I felt the same thing

That you wanted to kiss me
or that I wanted to kiss you?

Secret (o˘‿˘o)

Should we go grab a drink
after your meeting?

I might not get out until after 10...
Is that too late for you?

No, that's perfect

10:30 then? Ebisu station? I'll be
nearby

Cool

East exit

Ok, see you then

10:25. Ebisu station. East exit. Kana isn't here yet. I'm five minutes early. I'd like to sit down somewhere but there isn't a single public bench nearby. 10:30. 10:45. I wait. A signboard indicates its 2°C. I hop on the spot to warm myself up. 10:55. Still no sign of Kana. I go to the other side of the street so I can spot her coming. People everywhere. Afraid I might miss her. I go back to the stairs that lead up into the station. I wait. Lean against the lacquered brick wall. Yellow. Rub my hands. My forearms. 11:07. Still no sign of Kana. East exit. Ebisu station. I got it right. Ten times I reread our last exchange.

> 10:30 then? Ebisu station? I'll be nearby

> Cool

East exit

Ok, see you then

11:12. She doesn't want us to kiss. I should never have asked her. It was too blunt. She won't come. She could have at least sent me a message to cancel. Unless her meeting ran late. But so late on a Saturday? 11:18. Weird. Something must have happened. 11:31. I shouldn't have flirted with her.

11:44. I leave the station and start walking north, towards Shibuya, following the train tracks. But that's a ways. I stop in one of the bars that have popped up under the train tracks. Raw concrete. Dark. Loud. Veined wood bar. Ochre and yellow. Eight seats at most. Everyone standing. A typical place. And just as typically, the bartender, seeing me enter, shakes his hands, frantically repeating "no English." I tell him that I could leave if he doesn't want a foreigner inside but that I speak Japanese (a bartender's main job, in this kind of place, is to chat with the clients, which is why they usually refuse foreigners). He squints, eyeing me carefully, then reluctantly points out an open spot at the bar before turning to another customer. He sets down a plate of soft tofu topped with green onion and soya sauce in

89

front of the man. He comes back towards me, wipes the counter.

"Where did you learn to speak Japanese?"

"In Osaka."

"Wha! I grew up in Osaka."

"I love the Kansai accent. I was in Asahi, you?"

"Nishi."

"Very beautiful neighbourhood."

He smiles.

"You visiting Tokyo?"

"Actually, I was hoping to settle down in the area."

"Good. What can I get you?"

"O-nihonshu wo kudasai!"

A white tokkuri.

Full of very cold saké.

A china cup.

"Do you work in Tokyo?"

"Oh... Yes and no. I'm a writer."

"Wha! What do you write about?"

"I'm not quite sure yet. A novel about... Hmmm... Have you heard of Arai Suzuko?"

"You mean the artist, Arai Suzuko? I thought she was dead."

I clench my cup, pour myself another, and drink again.

"We used to live together."

"Who?"

"Arai Suzuko and me."

"Whaaoh! So you're the one who'd often be next to her on tv? I forgot she was with a foreigner..."

I feel my phone vibrate.

I pull it out of my pocket and place it on the counter. 12:38. The bartender takes a step back, his hands joined in front of his forehead.

"Please, I beg you most cordially, accept my sincerest condolences."

It's so sudden and so frank. I falter. He's looking at me. I'm going to cry. Or not. A knot in my stomach, that's all. He bows ceremoniously, his arms by his sides, before turning silently to another customer.

> Vincent! My meeting just ended! I'm so sorry! Are you still somewhere near Ebisu? I hope so... Let me know. I can be there in 10 minutes.

> I'm in a bar nearby. Come join me if you like.

> Be right there

91

It's the bar with no name
across from café Sarutahiko.
Easy to find. Just follow the
tracks northwards, on the
eastern side. I'll wait for you.

Kana. She comes in. Her eyelids almost black.

"So, how was the meeting?"

She doesn't say anything. We hug each other a little too intensely. She's embarrassed. Together we empty the tokkuri of saké, then I order beer, one after the other, as barely a word is spoken between us. Awkward. The need to kiss, maybe. American music. The train racing by every five minutes, shaking the bar. Beer bottles dancing. The bartender plants himself in front of us and kicks off the conversation. I feel like he wants to talk about Suzuko but holds himself back. He's probably assuming that Kana is my new girl-friend. Nothing he says is aimed at her though. The conversation between him and me leads nowhere. So I ask him as politely as I can to leave us alone, Kana and I. He looks astonished at first. Then offended. I didn't find the right words. He wipes the counter in front of us in a hurry before

93

turning towards someone else. A man. Thirties. Tie. Shirt.

And us. Two beers. Three beers. Four beers. Until we lose count. Her eyelids are blue now. Her phone shining brightly in her hands.

"We missed the last subway a while ago."

"Oh yeah. We did!"

"Taxis are crazy expensive at this time of night."

"It's alright, Kana, whereabouts do you live? I'm sure we can walk part of the way together."

"Oh no it'd be better to spend the night somewhere nearby."

She says it naturally. And just as naturally I say "ok let's do that" without really knowing what spending the night somewhere nearby means.

We pay.

We leave.

We buy cans of beer at the 7-Eleven.

Then she leads me through an incomprehensible mess of streets. Shibuya. Crowded like it were midday, but it's a surprisingly disorganized crowd. We weave our way through as best as we can. The pack of beer in my left hand. Heavy. My right hand, in Kana's. In her right hand, she's reviewing ratings for love hotels on her phone. "Lo-ve ho-tel-lu." That's how she pronounces it, one syllable at a time. In her thick Tokyo accent. The sweetness in her voice. I'm weak in the knees.

The love hotel Kana chose is at the end of a dark cul-de-sac. The entrance is lit by a single, slanted, pink neon, drilled into the wall above a sliding door. We enter. To the right, a large touch screen. To the left, a shelf full of plastic baskets filled with towels, soap and phosphorescent lube spray. Kana swipes the screen with a finger in search of a room that isn't too cheesy but there are only two candy-coloured rooms left, heart-shaped bed, ceiling mirror.

She books two hours, we grab a basket and take the tiny elevator, reeking of bleach, up to our floor.

A blinking lightbulb indicates which room is ours, at the far end of the hallway. We enter and the door locks automatically behind us. To unlock it you have to pay online. Otherwise you can't get out. Kana's the one who tells me that and I have to admit that I'm anxious. Will the door automatically unlock itself if there are tremors? It sobers me up a bit. What are we doing here?

Suzuko.

Ten seconds she's in my thoughts. Then the alcohol comes rushing back to my head.

On one of the walls a fake window opens up to a fake exterior. A television in the corner. Two fleshy mouths sucking on a pixelated penis. Reeks in here too. Kana turns off the TV with a flick of the finger. And we stand there facing one another, between the point of the heart-shaped bed and the bathroom door. Her eyelids are the colour of flesh again, vivid and smooth at the same time.

Kana slides her hands down my arms, from my shoulders to my wrists. She takes my fingers in hers. She holds them, feels them, as if sizing them up, gauging their weight, their temperature, before bringing them to her neck, to her cheeks, to her hot, oily eyelids. Are they covered in ointment?

"Are you ok?"

"No worse than usual."

Then she disappears into the bathroom.

I stretch out on the bed while I wait for her to come back. My head's spinning. I opt to lean with my back against the fake window, hands on my knees. Water running in the bathroom. I take off my sweater, my shoes, my belt. I pull back the comforter. Then put my sweater back on. I'm not quite sure what I should leave on, what I should take off. I lie facedown. On my side. On my back. I change my mind every two seconds. I start lowering my pants before pulling them back up just as quick. The water stops running in the bathroom. The muted friction of a towel. The creak of the door and the click of the light she turns off on her way out.

An alarm wakes us. I answer the love hotel's phone, stretching my arm over my head.

"Moshi moshi."

"Rooo... Vincent, who's calling at this time of night?"

"It's the housekeeper. She says that our two hours are up, that we have to leave now or pay for eight hours. What do you want to do?"

"Stay, obviously."

"Ok."

I hang up. We snuggle up again under the blankets. An animal smell. Our hair mixed together. Her nose buried in my neck. My lips against her eyelids.

We spend every night together three weeks in a row. Every time in a different love hotel. Her eyelids. They disturb me and upset me and scare me. All at once. When I'm at the apartment, during the day, I try to translate their beauty into words. Afternoon in Tokyo. A thousand rooftop reflections. The shimmering of the Sumida River. Ryōgoku Stadium. Kana. The city beyond the wall of glass. Fifteenth floor.

The clouds swell, shrink and disappear.

Suzuko hasn't reappeared once since I met Kana. It does me good and not so good. I feel sad and guilty. Suzuko. Gone. The gulf of her disappearance. I think of her. And I collapse. Into the kitchen chair. Facing the wall of glass. I try to recreate Suzuko's face, in my mind, but it's Kana's that appears. Her magnificent, obscene eyelids.

Captivating and swollen. Delightful sweets. Monstrous tumours. I struggle to sit up straight in my seat. 9:33 p.m. Already. Kana always writes to me before 10 to tell me which love hotel I can find her at. But I won't go tonight. I try to convince myself. There's nothing between her and me. It's just flirting, an unhealthy distraction. I close my eyes. I search a long time for Suzuko's face but I can't find it.

It's killing me.

9:46.

I wait for her text, trying to convince myself I'm not waiting. When she texts I'll tell her it'd be better if we didn't sleep together tonight, that I need to rest, to find myself again, to find Suzuko again. I don't know if she'll understand. Maybe she won't even write to me tonight. I might not have to explain anything to her. 10:05. 10:06. The night continues marching on minute by minute and, minute after minute, I get more and more worried, I can't help it. I'm afraid, always afraid that people will die. Now. I check my phone every thirty seconds. I wait. No danger. Everything's normal. Yes. I try to convince myself but it's hard. Something probably happened to her. I wait. I shouldn't. Anyways, I wanted to sleep alone in the apartment. Tonight. The idea suddenly seems completely absurd to me. Kana should write to me. Kana should've written to me. She always writes to me before 10 p.m.

10:09. Already.

The need to see her, to touch her, to meet her wherever she is. 10:10. I make a wish.

10:23.

> Hi Vincent, sorry, I'm writing you
> late.

> No worries. I wasn't waiting.

She gives me a time to meet at a love hotel in Shinjuku and I ride so fast to get there the city lights rip past me, leaving long multicolour streaks like in *Ghost in the Shell*.

Gallery 3331 is in the gym of what used to be an elementary school in Chiyoda. Ten metre high ceilings. Long lines of colour that once marked basketball, volleyball and handball courts on the hardwood floors. Hundreds of art pieces posted to the walls. On canvas or paper. Paintings and drawings and collages. Huge pieces and tiny pieces, produced by all kinds of artists. Professionals, amateurs, nobodies, celebrities, old people, young people, men, women. Someone hands me a piece of paper to note my ten favourite pieces on. A way to get visitors involved. I move through the room. February 24. Vernissage. Lots of people. I'll come choose my favourites some other time. Isn't worth the trouble tonight. The room is packed and Kana's eyelids, on the other side of the gallery, have got all my attention. Two damp, glistening wounds. Wounds to be treated. It's all I see. Then, a hand moves three or four times in front of my eyes. Big, dark fingers. I don't react right away. A beat. And another. Then I turn my head.

"Oh, hey, Pavle! I didn't notice you were there."

"I can see that. Were you daydreaming? What were you looking at?"

"Oh, nothing, uhh... It's just this exhibit... it's massive."

He squints in Kana's direction.

"Yeah, it is."

"How are you liking it?"

"It's pretty nice, actually. Almost a thousand pieces here. And they're all anonymous. It's impossible by sight alone to single out the professionals from the amateurs, the old from the young, the crazy from the... uhh... well... I mean... the results are what matters, only the results, not the context, not the artist's backstory. I love it."

"I wonder how the gallery managed to get so many pieces together. You would have needed an army for this."

"Well, I had to speak with at least six different people during the selection process."

"What!? Pavle, do you have a piece here? I didn't know that!"

"I'm sure you didn't, I didn't tell anyone."

"Ah... ok..."

"I even tried doing something different so my style wouldn't be so easy to pick out. The work for work's sake, not for ego, my career, the community, or the collector. It's actually quite liberating!"

Ayumi slips in between Pavle and me. Beaming. Black dress, colourful polka-dots. Hair in a bun. Long neck. Small golden earrings. She grabs us both by the arm.

"So how are you both finding the exhibit?"

"We were just talking about that actually. It's super nice!"

"It really is! But there's way too many people. I'll have to come back on a quieter day so that I can vote properly, but I don't know if I'll have the time..."

"We can come together."

"That'd be great. But this is all a bit much right now, I've had a long week... I think I'm going to head home. You think you guys could walk me to the subway?"

"I'm on my bike."

"Let's go have some beers, just the three of us, it's been a while, no?"

"Oh that's sounds nice, Pavle, but I came here to meet up with Kana tonight, and I haven't even spoken to her yet. I'm staying. I'm sure there's going to be a dinner, afterwards, with the gallery folk..."

Ayumi lowers her head, disappointment plain to see.

"Oh... I'm tired anyway, Vincent, I'm going home."

"You, Pavle?"

"Enh, I don't really feel like going out to eat with people I barely know tonight. I've had my fill of that recently."

"But you know Kana, Pavle!"

"Kana... no, I don't think so, who is she?"

"Haha! Well she knows you anyways."

"Ah, maybe she does, people *do* know who I am."

Pavle turns to Ayumi then.

"Shall we walk to the subway together?"

She lets go of my arm and hangs on to Pavle's with both hands.

"Oh, yes, let's go. We'll catch up soon, Vincent, ok?"

"Ok."

I say this with genuine enthusiasm but I feel rotten the moment the word leaves my lips. A part of me would have loved to have gone with Pavle and Ayumi.

"Don't worry, we'll find time to see each other soon."

They leave the gallery.

I'm still standing where they left me.

Kana still hasn't noticed I'm there. It's a bit strange. We had arranged a time to meet and everything. A piece of art has her captivated. Pavle's maybe. I'll give her some time to admire it. I drag my feet throughout the gym, waiting for her to notice me, but she never looks around her. But I do. It's all I do. Because every woman here has scarlet eyelids. Sudden realization. Embers. Something's up. But what? The dry air of the Tokyo winter. The wind, radioactive, coming from the north. An infection that's doing the rounds. It's all becoming muddled. I don't recognize anyone anymore. I rub my eyes. A skip in my heartbeat. Legs becoming heavy. Hushed conversation and laughter. Skirts and dresses and pants and dull leggings. The air surprisingly thick. Hard to breathe suddenly. Silhouettes in the gloom. Fiery eyelids by the dozen. Fireflies in the fog. My fog. In my gut and in my head and behind my pupils. Until it's opaque. Like ink. In my eyes. Hands. In front. Calm yourself. Calm myself. Breathe. Liquid. Ice. Stone. Impossible to swallow. Throat seizing up. Panic.

I get out of there.

In the hallway a broad sink like a horse trough, a row of fountains lined up next to each other.

I spray my face with cold water. Behind my ears and neck too. For a long time. It calms me a little. I'm breathing but I'm afraid. Afraid that it'll never be filled, the unbearable emptiness left by Suzuko. And yet. Suddenly a hand on the back of my neck. And almost instantly the air is clear and fresh once again.

"I'm here."

Her reassuring voice.
And the dread that disappears in two seconds.

Outside, the wind, deafening city noises. Flight of stairs and dead grass. The park in front of the old school. Old children's games, iron frames, faded colours. The seesaws looking like an Isamu Noguchi sculpture.

"Oh, Kana, thank you, I was having a hard time breathing in there. I'm feeling better now."

Her eyelids split in two by a line of black lashes. Her irises like holes. I lean against the low wall separating the street from the park. I still have a glass in my hand. Wasn't expecting that. I swallow a mouthful of wine as if everything was perfectly normal.

"Kana, you look like you were really enjoying the exhibit, you should go back."

"What, you already trying to get rid of me?"

She's laughing as she says it, unable to hold it back, her hands in front of her heart as if to protect it.

"No, of course not! I'm really happy to see you!"

"Let's go have some beers far from here, then!"

"There isn't going to be a dinner?"

"Uhh... Not that I'm aware of."

"Is there nothing more here at the vernissage that you want to see?"

She's laughing again.

"People come here to be seen and I've seen them."

"You sure?"

"Eeeh! You really do want to get rid of me, don't you?"

Shinbashi station. 11 p.m. Another bar under another rail line. Kana standing. Me next to her. Two glasses of beer on the counter in front of us. Her eyelids. Dull red in the dusky light. I want to touch them but I don't. She takes a sip of beer. Me too. A train passes by overhead. Bottles dancing on the counter. She drinks again. I do the same. It all plays out as though downing a bunch of beers in silence were just some kind of prelude to us piling our naked bodies on top of each other, later, in a love hotel. Loud music. Always touching, Kana and I. The tip of an elbow. The side of a thigh. The end of a finger.

None of the women around us have particularly colourful eyelids. People are letting themselves go. They're dancing between the bar tables, or rather they're bopping their heads to the rhythm of the music, or tapping a bottle, a foot, as if it's against the rules to move more than one body part at a time.

We down a couple of bottles in a row. Still at the counter, standing. Ever closer together. Her arms so thin. Our ribs rubbing against one another, up and down, every time she takes a breath. Standing too close together in public is frowned on. But if the bar is packed like this, it's not our fault. People eyeing us suspiciously. Clearly, I'm a foreigner. Some are staring at me. Unless it's Kana they're staring at. Jealousy or disapproval or desire in their eyes.

"Sorry, I really need to go to the bathroom."

Her voice crystalline. She leaves. A man who's clearly had too much to drink slides into her place at the bar.

"My friend'll be back in two minutes."

He completely ignores what I said. Maybe he thinks I spoke to him in English. Happens sometimes. He crosses his arms on the counter and buries his head in the middle as if to fall asleep. People tapping their bottles and feet a little louder. Sapphire Slows playing on the speakers. Kana comes back. Walking in synch with the music. A train passes by. Teeth-rattling vibrations, wall to wall. The building cracks a little. A fine mist of dry plaster falls from the ceiling, disappears in the cigarette smoke. I ask the man to please give Kana her spot back but he obviously

112

can't hear me. I put a hand on his shoulder. He doesn't react. Bah whatever. I step away from the counter carrying both glasses but he raises his head suddenly, knocks one of the beers, spilling it all down his back.

"Oh shit, sorry, I didn't mean to..."

The beer seeps into his jacket and into his pants. Disgusted, he wipes his neck with a few napkins then tries to look at me but his eyes can't focus on one spot. He flails his arm out (with the intention of pushing me, most likely) but falls face first on the floor. A thud. A few people turn to see what's happening. The guy grabs me by the ankles. He yanks hard. I fall backwards. The two glasses I was holding smash somewhere behind me. The sound of shattered windows. Hardwood floors. At least it isn't concrete. Smarts either way. Legs. Boots and shoes. I find Kana's. Turquoise and burnt yellow Pumas. I see them smash into the man's ribs a dozen times, trying to force him to let me go. Kana's foot cuts through the air, whistling like in a samurai film. People, laughing as they film the scene with their phones. Kana still kicking. I wiggle my legs but the man's got a tight grip. Kana kicks, and kicks, and kicks, the air tearing apart with every blow. More filming, more laughing. I admire Kana's tenacity. The man finally lets go of my ankles. Curls up on his side to protect himself. Kana hits him, and hits him, and hits him again, all control lost. Another woman joins the fray. The drunk's girlfriend most likely. She doesn't hit as fiercely as Kana but still. A little less laughter now. She's crazy, they say. They grab them from behind, her and Kana. Pin them to the floor next to me. Kana flings an arm around me. A dog pile on top of her. Her gasping breath on my face. Her bloody eyelids. Her fingers in my hair and in my mouth. Oh Kana. So tiny yet so strong. Four or five people to stop her. Another train passes by. Bottles dance. Other bottles sway, topple, roll off the table, one after another. Support beams cracking like twigs. Creases forming in the walls. It's not a train. People screaming. The counter a twisting snake. Light bulbs exploding in the ceiling. The floor dips a metre, rises another two, in fits. Our sprawled bodies flipped like pancakes. Customers rushing for the exit. Two bartenders try to get the drunk out before it's too late. They each drag him by an arm but the guy is heavy and limp and his clothes stick to the floor. I grab one of his legs and motion for Kana to grab the other. We're pretty buzzed ourselves. Doesn't stop us though, we manage to get the man out. Everyone outside now.

The bars are empty. The streets full.

Thousands of people gazing into their phones, silently, to see if they haven't missed an alert. The ground has stopped shaking. Kana hugs me tenderly. Short of breath. I hug her back. Shivers down my spine.

"Saved by an earthquake."

Her voice clear but winded. Kana. Her big, amused smile. Blood-smeared cheeks. I wipe it with my fingers. Just spreads it all out.

We go into a konbini. Blinding neons. Kana's white face. Red blood on her cheeks. I buy some wet wipes and a six-pack of saké. Kana moves behind the hot dog rolling machines so I can clean her face. Her head tilted slightly back. I wipe her forehead, her cheeks, her chin. Her suddenly pink skin. I change the wipe before focusing on her eyelids. Streaks of tiny turquoise veins, like a circuit of streams. I've never seen them in such vivid light before.

My left hand in her hair. In my right a third wipe, clean, which I use to dab. No sign of any cuts. On her face or her head. The blood has come from who knows where. I take out a fourth wipe. Carefully clear the crust from her eye-lashes, where the blood has congealed. Her eye-lids look more swollen than earlier. I think. Puffy like sunburn blisters.

"You ok? Are you hurt?"

"No more than usual."

"I don't see any cuts, you should be fine."

We leave the konbini. She opens a can of saké, we share it as we walk. The streets are even more crowded than they were ten minutes ago. Passersby, bottles in hand. Jackets unzipped. A festival atmosphere. Electronic music outside Shinbashi station. A man with headphones, behind a folding table. Laptop. Disk players. Vinyl. Amps. Tiny flashing lights. People gathered on the sidewalk, dancing as if the earthquake of the century were about to destroy Tokyo. Moving their bodies, for no real reason, at least once before dying.

Kana, me, the others. Arms flailing. And legs. The beat keeps coming back, pounding. In front of the station. Until two police officers get out of their car, chase the musician away, disperse the crowd to free up access to the subway. An excuse. The subway's been closed since midnight. They're flexing their muscles. People scatter into the street, block traffic. A man throws up at the base of a street lamp. A dog barks.

Kana opens a second can. We share it as we move away from Shinbashi station. The four remaining cans she carries in her left hand. With her right she hangs on to my elbow. She guides

117

me through the streets. On our way to some love hotel. We kiss under an overpass. Behind a garbage container. In a playground. Under the portico of a closed store. Until we wind up behind the Tomo museum. A tiny green, brown, muddy space, surrounded by scaffolding. Deserted at this time of night. We down the rest of the cans of saké sitting on a bench. Our legs intertwined. Cold hands in pants and up her skirt. The hard bench. The back of her neck. Her legs. Her fingers on my back. Shivers. Goosebumps. Cats' tongues. The cool air. The taste of saké in her mouth.

Easy to catch us. By surprise. Kana couldn't care less, me neither. We don't want to stop, our hands, our lips, everywhere. The smell of her hair. Scorched earth. Us. Stretched out on the bench. Feet in the air. Unstable. The empty cans of saké, abandoned, we'll collect them later. Our warm bodies imbibed with alcohol. The bench too narrow. We almost fall off. Kana plants a foot on the ground for balance, then stands up, pulls me to my feet. Her skirt comes down to an inch below her knees. The latest style. I hold her tight. We sway together, no hint of coordination. Impossible to let go of her though. Soft breeze. Early spring. 12 or 13°C. Want to take my clothes off. Smartest move to make given the circumstances. The thickness of our clothing. The thickest five millimetres in the world. Someone might see us. Buildings surrounding the park. An office building. Some twenty storeys, floor to

119

ceiling windows, all awash in darkness except one. A bright band of light. A woman walking across from left to right, the handle of a vacuum cleaner in hand.

Kana guides me to the building that's being renovated just ahead. We stumble a dozen times along the way. Trample on each other's feet. We laugh.

The scaffolding is covered in grey tarp. Bricks and rebar in the mud. Tarp flapping in the wind. Difficult to make out anything behind it. The perfect spot. For a homeless person looking for a quiet night. I think it over for a moment. Kana pushes me up against the scaffolding, grabs my shoulders, spreads my legs with her knees, presses her pelvis against mine. Her belly. Her breasts. My right hand behind her head. Such fine hair. A familiar smell of saliva and leather behind her ears. Her arm around my waist. Mine everywhere else. She lifts the edge of her skirt above her belly-button. Her thighs are freezing. Her little panties, so soft. She thrusts her fingers down my pants, unbuttons them, lowers them to my ankles. A bundle of fabric, no running away if we're caught. I think about that a moment. Just a moment. Her moans, and mine, under the scaffolding. The palm of my hand flat against her panties. I don't have a condom and I don't want to ask if she has one. No, most likely. Doesn't carry a purse. I don't care. It's good like this anyways. The delicate folds between her legs. My fingers. Her skin, so silky. A frenzy. Wanting it to go on forever. Almost in tears. Touching her, holding her against me. In case the earth opens up, swallows us both. Lose balance as if this evening's earthquake never ended. Like the earth, shaking nonstop since I got back to Tokyo. She wraps her arms around my waist. Her face nestled in my neck. Holds me hard, grinding herself on my hand. She trembles, goes tense. Her breath, maybe her last. Long and loud. Then she unclenches her fist and breathes, slowly, her chin against my collarbone. I can feel her. Something like wanting to love her. Rays of light shining through the tears in the grey tarp. Blinding strips of skin, petals on a dewy morning.

"You ok?"

"Yeah, you?"

"Yeah."

The urge to sleep. Right here. Under this scaffolding. To stay out here. Never go home. Sleep. I pull my pants back up, she lowers the edge of her skirt. And starts to climb the scaffolding. Without thinking twice I climb after her, all the way up, towards the eighth or ninth floor. The building has about a dozen. Only the outside is under renovation. We stare inside through a window, our hands flat against it. The red button of a coffee machine, the opal screen of a photocopier, computer lights pulsating, calm and constant. Sleeping beasts. Between the cubicles, in the dark. Easy to spot us. It's much brighter outside than in. The cloudy emerald-green ceiling. An alien brightness. The floor of the scaffolding, wood, as big as a double bed. We lie down on our sides, face to face, using our jackets as blankets. The bones of our hips and shoulders against the hard wood. Kana's eyelids puffier than I've ever seen them. Overly ripened figs, split open, juicy. Magnificent. More than that. Sublime. The wave that breaks the ship in the distance. Terrible and fascinating. The feeling of security. A nuclear explosion on television. Her eyelids. Wounds. They tie my stomach in knots. I'm going to cry. No. Scared stiff. Can't breathe. Scared to lose. Afraid she's hurting. Afraid I'm hurting too.

Kana isn't smiling anymore. Her hands under her head like a pillow. I bring my fingers to her swollen, barely open eyelids. I rub them. They're burning hot.

"What happened to your eyes, Kana?"

"Oh Vincent, you know."

"What do I know?"

"Oh... It's not easy... To get through something, you have to forget what's causing you so much pain. I can see that... But we don't forget, ever, we bury. And that's no help at all. So... remember... Remember Suzuko, go back to the beginning and you'll... you'll understand, in the end."

2

When I saw her walk into the bookstore on March 11, 2016, she looked like she was trying to figure out why there were so many people. She took a step back, timid.

"Everyone's welcome, you can stay."

She frowned and said "I no understand, I sorry" with an unmistakable Japanese accent. Then stuck her tongue out, as though there was nothing else to be done.

"I just said that you could stay, no problem. But there isn't much going on... to be honest..."

Her eyes and mouth opened wide.

"Eeeh! You speak Japanese?"

"A little."

"How?"

"Oh I learned it at university... At first because I liked the books by Ogawa Yōko... And I taught English for three years in Osaka. You could say I got a lot of practice... Wasn't too long ago that I lived there."

"Eeeh!"

"I lived in Asahi, near the river."

"Sorry... I don't really know Osaka, I'm from Tokyo."

"Oh I'd like to..."

I never got the chance to finish that sentence though, my publisher was gently tugging on my sleeve.

"Microphone's ready, I'd like you to come talk about your book for a bit."

"In five minutes, ok?"

"Hmmm... There's barely any alcohol left, people are going to start leaving soon..."

She walked away.

"What is this?"

"It's a book launch... But people mostly come to drink free wine."

"Eeeh!"

"Would you like a glass?"

"I'd love one."

"I'm Vincent, by the way."

"I'm Suzuko."

We bowed a little towards each other, smiling.

"And what brings you to Montreal?"

"I'm visiting."

"For how long?"

"I'm leaving tomorrow evening for Toronto."

"You should stay in Montreal, it's more fun."

"Eeeh, I'd like to! But I have to go back to Tokyo. I have a new contract that starts Monday."

"Oh what kind of contract?"

She looked around her, not answering.

"Sorry, I'm nosy."

"No, don't worry about it. I'm a hakusei-shi."

I blinked. She laughed.

"Eeeh... it's normal that you don't know what that means, it's not something you hear every day."

My publisher came over to us again. Spoke to Suzuko.

"I'm sorry, my dear."

"She speaks Japanese, Olga."

"Ah, ok, well. I didn't know you brought someone back with you from Japan."

"No, she just came into the bookstore, we just met."

"Ok, anyways, it's time to start talking about your book. Come on, let's go."

"Just one more minute, this won't take long."

She sighed. Then left to find something to drink.

"Which part of Tokyo do you live in?"

"Sumida. Near Morishita station."

"How many stations are there in Tokyo? Ten thousand? Morishita, I don't know it."

She downed the rest of her wine. I did the same. Then my publisher came back, beer in hand, more determined than ever.

"It's time."

"Ten seconds, Olga."

She pretended not to hear me. She turned to Suzuko.

"Look, you seem like a nice girl, my dear, but Vincent has things to do right now."

That made me laugh.

"Ok, Olga, one second."

"No, let's go, the bookstore's emptying out."

"Alright... I have to go."

"Ok."

"But maybe we could grab breakfast together, tomorrow? I need to practice my Japanese, I'm sure it's all Greek to my publisher."

"Haha, you speak really well though."

"Nah, I don't even know what hakusei-shi means. You'll have to explain it to me. You think we could meet here, in front of the bookstore, tomorrow around ten o'clock?"

"Eeeh! That sounds good."

Olga sighed. Completely discouraged.

"Alright, I'm coming."

"Why did you even come back to Montreal, Vincent?"

"Sorry, I'm really happy to be here tonight, I swear."

"Could've fooled me."

"Oh don't think like that. I'm sorry, honestly. It's just I don't know most of these people. It... it's not easy, my head's somewhere else."

"Not just your head."

"Sorry."

"Hey, isn't it a Japanese thing to apologize after everything you say?"

"Sorry."

She laughed.

"Alright, go!"

We bought bagels and cream cheese on Fairmount before going to find a bench in Lahaie Park. Disemboweled plastic bags scattered on muddy grass. Suzuko was taking pictures of the squirrels and there was a lingering smell of freshly thawed dog shit. The remnants of brown snow around the edges of the pathways. Cigarette butts, gravel, wet Kleenex.

"I looked up what hakusei-shi means when I got home last night."

"Oh yes? How do you say it?"

"Taxidermist."

"Oh that's pretty."

"Have you been one for a long time?"

"Since I was very little. My father taught me. He used to stuff people's pets. I was never really a big fan of that. I mean... people wanting to go on living with the corpse of their dog, their cat, their gold-fish, as if they're still alive... That's pretty grim."

"Is there a lot of demand for that in Tokyo?"

"Surprisingly, yes. When I opened my own workshop, my father wanted to send some clients my way. I refused, he insisted, and then he died."

She said it so abruptly. I didn't know what to say back. She took a bite of her bagel. A squirrel hopped towards her.

"I'm sorry, how long ago?"

She chewed for at least a minute before swallowing.

"Five and a half years."

Distractedly she tossed a piece of the bagel to the squirrel but it was more interested in snacking on an old Kleenex.

"So did you end up taking on his customers?"

"Who? My father's? I tried to... but it didn't really work out. I was stuffing the animals exactly the way they were bringing them to me. Twisted, stiff, eyes half open, bulging. Looking dead, basically. I don't know what had gotten into me. My father's customers didn't really appreciate it, I mean..."

"I can imagine."

"My father had just died and they wanted me to bring their cats back to life? Seriously? Was I to go on living like nothing had happened, with my dad sitting there at the kitchen table, embalmed in front of a bowl of noodles?"

Then she turned and looked at me as if her question wasn't purely rhetorical.

"Uhh... yeah, that would be weird."

"So so, no one brings me their pets to stuff anymore. I restore pieces for natural history museums now. But I'd rather work on other things."

She smeared the rest of her bagel in the cream cheese container sitting on the bench between us, lost in her thoughts.

"For a while, I was going to the pound."

She brought the bagel up to her mouth but stopped before biting into it.

"I used to collect the animals they'd just put down. The animals that were too old, or too sick, or were suffering too much to be saved. And I would stuff them just as they were: frail and sickly."

I dipped a bagel into the cream cheese container too. Three scrawny pigeons limped towards us. Suzuko tossed them a few morsels (which they each lost a few feathers over).

"It's better not to feed the animals."

"Oh."

"These cast-offs that you stuffed... Did you sell them?"

"Eeeh... They just piled up in my workshop for months. Actually, it was a little creepy. But what can you do, I still had restoration work for museums. Still have to earn a living."

She held an arm out to pet a dog that was walking by, but its owner pulled on the leash, preventing the animal from eating the rest of Suzuko's bagel.

"I teach a little and write novels for a living."

"Oh!"

"Yesterday was the launch for my second novel actually."

"Eeeh! Why didn't you tell me?"

The pigeons came back to peck at the sesame seeds that had fallen at our feet. One of them only had stumps for feet. It was the most combative of the trio. Suzuko said "I really like that one" pointing at it as if it were the cutest bird in the world. I laughed.

"So what did you end up doing with the cast-offs?"

"Ono Ayumi, a friend of mine, had just opened a contemporary art gallery. Actually, deep down I had put together a weird collection in the hope that it might interest her. I brought her to my workshop to show her, and after that... she was my work's biggest fan. I was so happy! Together we organized my first exhibit in her brand new gallery."

"That's really cool."

"Oh yes! But oh no! Eeeh!"

She was looking upset.

"What is it, Suzuko? Did I say something wrong?"

"No, it's me. I've been talking about my life this whole time. I'm sorry, it's so rude."

"No, not at all."

"Forgive me..."

"I don't care if it was rude or not, I'm just glad to be here talking with you, really. I've thought about Japan every day since I got back to Montreal. It's bad, hasn't even been two months... Are you going to do another exhibit in Tokyo? I'd really love to see what you do."

"Oh... I've already used the same concept twice. It was quite a success, Ayumi would love for me to do it again... But I'd be repeating myself, and that's boring."

"I understand."

"Now I do performance pieces. Well, I did one before coming to Canada, but I want to do more."

"What kind of performance?"

Suddenly she looked embarrassed. She wiped her mouth with a napkin even though there was nothing there to wipe.

"It's hard to explain... I used a bear head... But uhh... well I'll show you if you ever come to Tokyo."

Two weeks later I flew to Tokyo and Suzuko invited me, that same night I arrived, to a vernissage for a Taiwanese artist. I left my suitcase in the tiny basement studio of some random building I rented at the last minute, not far from Ono Gallery, in Ginza. I took a shower and left.

Suzuko was waiting for me in front of the glass door to the gallery, her right shoulder leaning against the steel frame. She hastily smoothed out her skirt when she saw me arrive.

"Oh I'm happy to see you."

We went in. The acidic lighting irritated the eyes. We cleared a path through the crowd to the centre of the gallery, walking side by side, where stood a woman in an ochre and gold dress, so loose and breezy it looked like fire.

"This is Ono Ayumi."

"Very pleased to meet you."

"Likewise."

Ayumi took both my hands into hers as she spoke to Suzuko.

"You know, people can't stop talking to me about your last performance, we really can't wait for the next one."

"I'm working on it."

Then Ayumi looked me straight in the eye without letting go of my hands.

"Suzuko told me you published an essay on Sophie Calle. I love Sophie Calle!"

"Uhh... Suzuko spoke to you about me?"

"Of course she did."

Silence.

"Oh don't be embarrassed, you two."

She bowed her head slightly and let go of my hands, gently.

"Vincent, while I'm thinking about it... if ever you'd like to write an article about Li Yi-Fan's installation, that'd be wonderful. He's a promising artist. I could arrange a meeting this week, if you're interested."

"I'd love to but I mostly write fiction... and in French too..."

"I see... Well, take your time looking at the exhibit. The head of a contemporary art magazine in France—*Initiales*—is a good friend of mine. I wrote my thesis in London and Paris. I could put you in touch with her."

"You speak French?"

"Oh no, no, no, not at all! I only know how to say *'voulez-vous coucher avec moi?'*"

"Well... that's a start."

"Haha. Why don't you join us for dinner after the vernissage? I'd love that. We'll be about eight or nine people."

I looked at Suzuko.

She looked embarrassed by the invitation but didn't say no.

Li Yi-Fan was in his early twenties. Jeans and shirt. Mao hairdo. And looking unsettled by the fact that his vernissage had attracted so many people. To steady his nerves he was drinking beer, can after can, which he would open with the tip of a pocket knife. It almost looked like it was a performance piece (you never know with this kind of crowd). In his left hand he held the can, firmly, in his right the knife which he thrust into the aluminum with one swift strike.

And what was always going to happen happened.

Li Yi-Fan opened up his left wrist from one side to the other.

The can fell to the ground. The DJ turned up the music. People turned to look at Li. There was a brief moment of amazement. Blood pissing out like in the final scene of *Sanjuro* (a Kurosawa film that Li was actually in the middle of quoting).

The photographers, wielding cameras with over-size lenses, snapped away at the blood spurts. Everyone else was filming with their phone. But the blood didn't gush for long. There were no special effects. Li wrapped his right hand around his left. Blood all over his shirt, his pants, the floor. Li on his knees. The crowd around him uneasy. A mix of surprise, curiosity, concern. Li lying on the ground, unconscious. The crowd dumbstruck. White walls. Ayumi kneeling in the puddle of warm blood. The fiery dress soaked to the fringes. Li obviously had not spoken to her about a performance.

So, no dinner after the vernissage. Ayumi left with Li Yi-Fan in the ambulance. And everybody left the gallery with the impression they'd witnessed something powerful. But had it been art? Or did Li just slice into his wrist by accident? Accident or not, did it really matter, in the end? One way or another, the esthetic experience had been extremely intense, no? We discussed it, Suzuko and I, as we walked along Shōwa Avenue, and, I could already tell, I was happy to be in Japan, even if only for three weeks.

The buildings were slender, bright, bathed entirely in a soft, soothing white light. And I was exhausted but excited by the idea of spending the rest of the evening alone with Suzuko.

We turned down a small street to the left, narrow, dark, without sidewalks.

"So, do you think you'll write an article about the exhibit? I'm sure there's lots to say on accidents in contemporary art..."

"Maybe... but accidents like that one, there must be hundreds of them every day and no one questions whether it's art or not, no?"

"Eeeh! And the reference to Kurosawa? Do you think that was just a coincidence?"

"I don't know. Hmmm... Maybe... Those holes they cut right into the gallery walls, did you take a peek in them? I think *that* was supposed to be the exhibit..."

"I didn't have time."

"Me neither. If I'm to write even a half decent article I'll have to go back to the gallery before I head back to Montreal. Do you think your friend could arrange an interview with Li sometime in the next few days?"

"If he survives."

"Haha."

"It's not funny."

"Oh yeah, no, of course not. It was a nervous laugh, sorry."

We continued down the tiny street without sidewalks into an industrial park, which was wedged in between Tsukiji (the fish market which just announced it would be moving) and the Hama-rikyū Gardens.

Brick buildings, off-white. Smashed window panes. The remains of a rusty crane. Cars coasting by, lazily, sketchy silhouettes on the street corners. Waterproof jackets and rain boots. A frantic hubbub around the dumpsters. Huge crows picking apart garbage bags. The air thick with humidity on our shoulders. What the hell were we doing in an industrial park in the middle of the night? A forklift zipped back and forth between two warehouses while a group of men stood out front chain smoking. Suzuko fished a card out of her shoulder bag and waved it in front of a graffiti-covered garage door that opened, slowly, with a horrible metallic grinding.

"Come in, welcome."

The place was awash in darkness. Suzuko marched in with confidence. I followed her blindly. The garage door closed behind me. Brief click. Electric crackling. Then with a flash two rows of neons lit up in the ceiling.

And I saw.

The place was teeming with animals. Dozens and dozens of them. Birds, rodents, cats, mammals, amphibians. Everywhere. Their eyes shining in the fluorescent neon. Their fur, their feathers, quivering from the ventilation. A doe sniffing in the garbage can. Three pelicans gazing out a window pane, their necks craned, wings spread. Two hares looked poised to jump from one stool to another. Two otters were sleeping curled up under the tables, their fur coats glistening like they'd just been in water. You could hear the flow of a stream somewhere in the distance, leaves fluttering in the wind. Or almost.

Suzuko wandered among the animals, rubbing them each behind the ear, under the beak, along their neck.

"A contract for the National Museum of Nature and Science in Tokyo."

"It's magnificent."

"Thanks but I'm just restoring their collection. I don't find it that interesting."

She stopped to the right of a wolf. Massive. Sitting. Big grey paws. White breast. Savage snout. Empty eyes (two black marbles were lying between its paws, next to a half-chewed field mouse).

"It's just food on the table."

"The field mouse?"

"What? Oh no. I mean, this kind of contract I do for the museums, it puts food on the table."

She looked depressed suddenly.

"All of these animals... The only one I'm proud of is this little mouse here, the gutted one, you see? The others look too lifelike. It's too fake."

The face of the eyeless wolf was frightening. Suzuko kept her hand on the animal's head as if to keep it from pouncing at me.

"Would you like a drink?"

"I'd love one."

I sat on a stool, trying to avoid the wolf's empty gaze. Suzuko went to get a bottle of whisky from a cupboard mounted to the wall above an industrial sink and, from the freezer to the right, she fished out two ice cubes which she tossed into two glasses.

"Kampai."

I took a sip. My gaze then fell on a bear's head, which was resting on a metal shelf next to some frogs.

"You spotted the bear head..."

"Yes... It's beautiful..."

I took another sip of whisky.

"The director of a regional museum sent it to me. The remains of a car accident. He kept it in a freezer for months and didn't really know what to do with it. I emptied it out to conserve it better."

"In Montreal I remember you were telling me about a performance... Was it with that bear head?"

She thought it over.

"I'll show you if you like."

She downed the rest of her whisky as if it were water. I downed mine, burning my throat. Then she went to get the bear head, which we pulled over her head, together.

"Careful, yes like that. So so, ok. You can let go now, thanks."

"Where are the holes for your eyes?"

"There are none. The bear's eyes don't line up with mine. I'd have to cut holes in its throat if I want to see anything... And that'd be a little scary, an animal with four eyes, no?"

Behind the snout, Suzuko's voice was deep.

I took a step back.

The bear head covered half her shoulders. At first Suzuko steadied it with both hands, until she found the right spot to balance it. Then she bent her knees slightly before she held her arms out in front of her, blindly.

"Come closer."

Her voice cavernous. The bear's maw. Suzuko's clammy fingers which I delicately touched with the tips of mine. Right away she held them, felt them, as if sizing them up, gauging their weight, their temperature.

She grabbed me by the wrists, pulled me gently towards her until our chests, our bellies, our thighs were touching.

The bear's snout in my face. Coarse fur. Dry nose. A smell of saliva and leather. My fingers holding her shoulder blades. Delicate like the wings of a hummingbird. Her arms wrapped tight behind my back. This must be part of the performance. She said "I'll show you" so

149

now she was showing me. The enormous bear head. The breathing within. A hacking, choking sound. She must be suffocating in there. The thought crossed my mind as I tried to stay focused on the performance. But I was finding it difficult. I was concerned. Afraid of hugging Suzuko too tightly. Or not tightly enough. Or the wrong way. I was afraid she might be getting bored. Was that a sigh just now? Guttural noises from the maw. Her belly rising and falling. Then, little twitches in her abdomen, as if she were coughing.

She was gasping for air, she had to be.

I let her go.

"Already?"

Hoarse voice.

"Sorry, I was afraid you'd..."

"Everything ok, Vincent?"

"Yeah, yeah, you?"

I helped her take the bear head off. Red cheeks covered in sweat, skin marked by the rough interior of the head. Gasping.

"I'm going to have to... widen the air shafts."

I was thinking I should have hugged her longer, that I wanted more. I held my arms out to her so that we could hold each other once again but she just stood there unmoving, her arms hanging limply by her sides.

And I felt stupid.

The performance was over.

Not once did we see each other in the three weeks that followed. The restoration work for the National Museum of Nature and Science occupied all her time, which is why Suzuko asked one of her friends, Pavle Jovovic, to get in touch with me. He texted me so we could arrange a time to meet in front of the statue of Takamori Saigō and his dog.

Noon. Ueno Park.

Crowded. I recall. The clickety-clacking of getas on the cement surrounding the statue. Groups of women having their pictures taken. Peace signs, heads tilted to the side, dainty smiles. And this guy emerging from the lot of them. Towering. Shirt, pattern undefined. Black jeans. Burly. Fuzzy mane. A bandit's toque placed on the top of his head. Ring dangling from his nose.

And earlobes with holes so big you could pass a 100 yen coin through them.

"Hi, you wouldn't happen to be Pavle Jovovic, would you?"

"Oha! You must be Vincent, pleased to meet you!"

He had a welcoming voice, spoke Japanese like he was Tokyo born and bred. I bowed to greet him. He didn't. He grabbed me in his arms, squeezed me tight for a moment. Then we began to walk down the wide, busy pathway.

Cherry trees, heavy with white flowers. Soft, green grass. Women in yukatas, some of them wearing more sophisticated kimonos.

"Suzuko tells me you're a writer."

"Oh you were talking about me?"

"Bah just a little."

He laughed.

To the left of an old Buddhist temple we turned and began descending a set of stone stairs.

"Suzuko seems really busy with her taxidermy... I bought my plane ticket on a whim, maybe I should have waited and came to Tokyo after her contract was done."

"Nah. This is the best time of year to visit the city. Freezing barely a month ago, and we'll be roasting alive a month from now."

"I could have at least..."

"Don't worry, Suzuko always works a lot, anyways. If you came some other time, wouldn't have made a difference."

"Alright, well either way, I'm glad she introduced us. I would probably have gone there to annoy her, I wouldn't have been able to stop myself."

"Haha, for that you'd have to know where her workshop is."

"I do know where it is, she took me there, after Li Yi-Fan's vernissage."

His eyes shot open and his arms flew up.

"You serious? You went to her workshop?"

"Uhh... yeah... why?"

When we reached the bottom of the stairs Pavle turned right, a little abruptly. I followed him. Suddenly he was walking quite quickly.

"Suzuko and I have been friends for ten years now and she's never invited me there! How long have you two known each other?"

"Uhh... we had breakfast together once in Montreal about a month ago. We wrote to each other a bit since then, but that's it."

Pavle, desperation on his face, gave his head a good rub. Two swan-shaped paddle boats floated peacefully in the creek next to us.

"Vincent, I don't know what's going on between Suzuko and you, but treat her well, please."

It really looked like I wouldn't be seeing Suzuko again before flying back to Montreal. At least, when she suggested that I come spend my last evening in Tokyo with her at her workshop, I had already given up hope.

The place was full of mounted animals, like the last time, but their positions in the room had changed. They were lined up in rows at the back of the main room, like students in a class waiting for their school photo to be taken. New clothes and fresh haircuts. The little guys in front (rodents and amphibians), medium-sized animals in the middle (birds of prey, small felines), and the biggest in the back (an ostrich and a few tall, four-legged animals). Only the wolf sat apart, sitting in front of one of the support columns. Chest out. A thick fur coat. Mouth open. Eyes black and sad. Soon, some employees from the museum would be coming, to wrest him and the other animals from Suzuko.

Suzuko.

She was wearing old khaki coveralls and a stained jacket. No shower, no change of clothes. No particular effort on her part just to please me. I was wearing my nicest clothes. Pale blue chino pants and a t-shirt with a skull and cross-bones screen print by an artist from Osaka. We clashed. But that was ok, I had pretty much convinced myself that nothing would happen, romantically speaking, between Suzuko and me. Otherwise she would have found the time to see me sometime between arriving and leaving Tokyo.

"Would you like a glass of whisky?"

"Please. It was really excellent last time."

"Oh, I finished that bottle a few days ago. This is a new one today. Suntory. A little harsher, sorry, it's commercial whisky."

She went and took a bottle out of the cup-board, opened the small freezer, took out two ice cubes, which she tossed into two glasses, before pouring in the whisky. We stood in the kitchen, hips leaning against the counter.

"Where did you come up with the idea for that performance you showed me the other night?"

She took a sip of whisky.

"When I got the bear head I... I didn't know what to do with it right away. I just emptied it out so it would keep, like I told you. And then... I had a dream that night."

She took another sip of whisky. I took one too. The alcohol made my tongue tingle, like she said it would, before burning my throat.

"In my dream, I was here, in my workshop, and the bear, over there under the window, but whole, you know, plump body." She imitated the bear by arching her back, standing on her toes, her arms outstretched, her legs bent and her cheeks puffed out. "He was standing on his hind legs."

"I see."

"His front legs, he was holding them out towards me, like this, so... so I moved closer, timidly... and... I... I remember, in my dream... it's weird... I was afraid but the bear looked friendly, I desperately wanted it to wrap me in its arms. I moved closer, until I was snuggled up against his rib cage."

She moved her glass from her right hand to her left.

"He was massive, and I was tiny, in comparison. His paws surrounded me, and I tried to wrap my arms around him, tightly but tenderly, like he was doing, but they were too short, my hands barely reached his back. I grabbed a fistful of fur and pulled him closer to me. I could feel skin shifting under the fur. I could feel the muscles in his flanks against my forearms, the sturdiness of his paws on my shoulders."

She set her glass down next to the sink. Like a small iceberg, the ice cube floated in the whisky. She went and got the bear head and placed it on the counter. Instinctively, I scratched it behind the ear.

"I can remember there was a moment when I was telling myself it wasn't normal to be hugging a bear, that it was actually very dangerous. But it was already too late. And that's what woke me up, I think, the thought that it might be dangerous. But there was no reason to be afraid. I felt safe in his arms."

I took a second sip of whisky.

"The idea for my performance stems from that dream: I'd stand there in the middle of the gallery, wearing the bear head, hold out my arms, and wait for the visitors to come to me."

She lifted the bear head by its jowls. I helped her to balance it on her shoulders.

Then she held her arms out.

I took her hands.

"In the middle of the gallery..." Her voice was cavernous now. "Every time someone started hugging me... I wondered how long they would need before they pushed me away, how long the dream would go on for before it faded."

I didn't return to Montreal the next day as planned. I extended the lease for the tiny studio in Ginza. It was neither modern nor charming. A single bed filled almost the entire space. A worn rope carpet on the floor. The ceiling so low I walked around with my head tilted to the side. There was also a two-in-one toilet and shower that had the only window in the apartment. Its opening was level with a shopping street. I would watch feet and calves pass by. And dogs and cats and crows. Felt like I was having a shower in the middle of the sidewalk.

Despite it all I loved that apartment. It was cheap. In the middle of Tokyo. Not far from Suzuko's workshop.

I started tutoring English, to the son of an architect couple Pavle introduced me to. I had no working visa, but I didn't charge a lot. The couple recommended me to a colleague of theirs, who recommended me in turn. I quickly found myself teaching twenty hours a week. Always in extravagant houses, lit up day and night.

I didn't love teaching English but the work gave me a lot of free time to write, which I forced myself to do every morning, lying face down in bed. The rest of the morning I would take long walks through the city, making a mental map of it, and in the evenings I would go visit Suzuko in her workshop. The collection for the National Museum of Nature and Science was long gone. A dozen pink flamingoes now filled it. A restoration contract for Isetan, a department store in Shinjuku.

The evenings we spent together in the workshop usually played out the same. We'd talk. We'd drink whisky. We'd drink some more. We'd drink even more. She could hold her alcohol better than me. Sooner or later she would grab the bear head, and we would struggle to balance it on her shoulders. We would undress, awkwardly, and hold each other tightly and tenderly. Her skin clammy, then wet, then dripping. Bands of gleaming pink stretching out over her body. Feathers hanging in the air all around us. Pink. All those flamingoes, lifeless. Dead. Their wings pulled off. Necks broken. Suzuko and I sprawled out on a table or on the icy concrete floor. Her body glistening in the neon light. The wobbly bear head and Suzuko's throaty wheezing inside. The dark areolas of her breasts. The stools. The pots of glue and the scissors. I would have loved to see her face, when we made love, but that was out of the question. Without the bear head Suzuko refused to be touched.

At first I found our way of making love to be a little strange, to say the least. But as the weeks passed I got used to it. Of course, the bear head was heavy, cumbersome, and Suzuko would always end up gasping for air inside it. It wasn't the perfect system. Despite Suzuko expanding the air channels, the air never flowed unobstructed through the muzzle. And she was blind with it on. But it suited us both that our sex life had so clearly been separated from the rest of our relationship. There was a time for talking. A time to see friends. A time to undress, to touch, to make love. Things were clear.

More or less.

Suzuko told me about how when she was little she would often wear the animal heads lying around her dad's workshop. Those were the only moments he let himself take her in his arms, cradle her, nuzzle her neck. He never doted on her otherwise. The animal heads pushed father and daughter away from each other, yet also created the conditions to bring them closer together. Suzuko would feel protected. She would feel strong. She would feel real. She would feel free. It could never last forever, however. Once Suzuko was a teenager, her father found it improper to indulge an animal-headed girl. He tossed away all the animal heads in his workshop, and no one ever took Suzuko in their arms again.

No one.

Until her first performance.

I was in the middle of writing, lying on my belly, when I got a message from Suzuko.

Can you come to my workshop?

Now?

Yes!!!

You ok? What's wrong?

It's just I kinda feel like...
Oh it's a surprise!

Ok, I'm on my way. Be there in 20 mins.

Suzuko had never asked me to come see her at her workshop so early in the afternoon. I abandoned my computer, leaving it open on the bed halfway through a sentence. I took a quick shower, got dressed, and hopped on my bike. And I rode. As fast as I possibly could. Shōwa-dori. Harumi-dori. Two wide streets lined with skyscrapers. Right until the fish market. I turned right. Mopeds laden with mountains of Styrofoam boxes were making the rounds between the port and the local restaurants. One of the first sweltering days of May. Sloshing around in their own sweat, men in long, yellow raincoats, armed with white and red batons, were trying to choreograph the flow of pedestrians, reefer trucks, and forklifts. Apparently to little success. I was riding on the bike path, just barely avoiding a collision more than three times before taking a left, down the narrow, potholed street which led to Suzuko's workshop.

Storage lots. Sheet metal roofs. Dumpster bins. A mere leap and a jump from the chic Ginza neighbourhood. Tokyo's crazy. I could ride here nonstop, night and day, without ever becoming bored.

I leaned my bike against a dry, puny tree. A leaf or two, maybe. I took my helmet off and tousled my hair a bit so it wouldn't look so flat. And knocked on the garage door, which opened, slowly, grinding ever upwards, like in a Muranishi film, revealing, little by little, Suzuko in her steel toe boots, the tops of her calves, bare, her perfect

167

knees, small and round, her white thighs, torn shorts, work coat, her cat-like shoulders, her neck, her slightly chapped lips.

"Whisky?"

"Uhh, ok, but isn't it a little early to start drinking?"

She smiled, beaming.

"Eeeh! What's up? You look upset... You ok?"

"Yeah I'm ok, sorry... It's just hot out and I rode fast, I really wanted to see you."

"I wanted to see you too! I have something to show you, come."

She was skipping as she led me by the arm, excited like a little girl on vacation.

"The guys from Isetan came to pick up all the flamingoes I've been restoring these last few weeks. I'm free!"

I looked around, suddenly worried. The workshop was completely bare. Not one feather. Not one hair.

"The... the bear head, I... Did they take that too?"

169

"Eeeh! What are you talking about? The bear head is mine, obviously! I just put it away... for the moment..."

Then she blushed as she retrieved a bottle from the cupboard over the sink.

"I've been keeping this for a special occasion. Aged fifty years."

"Wow."

She took out two glasses, put an ice cube in each, poured the whisky in. A well-established ritual. The way she handled the glasses, the ice cubes, the bottle. Perfect form. Second nature.

"I always put ice in my whisky, sorry. I put some in yours, that ok?"

"Oh yeah, sure."

"What did you do this morning?"

"Uhh... Typed a little on my keyboard. And uhh... that reminds me... I have to warn you..."

"What?"

"I started this thing... a novel where most of the story takes place here, in Tokyo. I talk about you, the workshop, us... It's a little autobiographical. Is that ok with you?"

"Ah... oh... sure... Are you writing this story in Japanese?"

"My writing in Japanese is only good enough for texting."

"But I won't be able to read your book if you write it in French!"

"This isn't going to be published any time soon, that'll give you time to learn."

"Give me ten years."

"Hahaha!"

"In the meantime, kampai!"

We took a few sips in silence, standing next to the counter. The smell of seaweed and green tea.

"Didn't you want to show me something?"

"Eeeh! Yeah!"

She skipped to the other end of the workshop, the glass of whisky still in her hand, and pranced back again, a little box under her arm, which she put on the counter, all smiles. From the box, she took out a tuft of red and white fur, which she clutched tightly to her chest for a moment before handing it to me.

Never in all my life have I touched anything so soft. Such fine hair. So light. Supple like the most delicate silk.

"I found this fox at the pound this morning. The employees picked it up on the banks of the Sumida, behind the fish market. That's what they told me. I often ride down that way to get to the workshop. It's really close by. I wonder how the fox made it all the way here... She was probably hit by a reefer truck. There's so much traffic around the market, especially in the morning, it's so dangerous!"

I examined the animal more closely. Its hind legs mangled. Its pelvis flattened. But otherwise the fox appeared no worse for wear. Its long, fluffy tail looked to have been spared by the accident, its muzzle too.

"What do you have planned for this fox, Suzuko?"

Three days later Suzuko asked me to meet her in Sumida, at 7, in a paved square. Got there at 6:40. A ginkgo in the centre. Fan-shaped leaves. Half the square shaded. No wind. No birds. A sign pointing out the location of emergency materials, in case of earthquakes.

A tabby, its tail straight up, was slowly crossing through the square, totally unperturbed by my presence. Suzuko rolled up from the bike path that runs alongside the canal. She braked then placed a foot on the ground as she looked at her watch.

"I'm early, have you been waiting for me for long?"

"No, not at all, two minutes at most."

The cat lazily rubbed her calf as she passed by. She patted its back for a second. It continued on its way.

"I live here, just over there, you see? Behind the pink building, on the fifteenth floor (her face flushed). You want to come up?"

She gently repositioned the backpack hanging from her shoulder. She had never invited me up to her place before.

Fifteenth floor.

She turned the key in the lock. Pulled on the handle. And we went into her apartment. A bright little cocoon despite the coming dusk. I went over to the wall of glass and the floor began to shake.

Two interminable seconds. Suzuko never flinched.

"Did you feel that earthquake?"

"What? When?"

"Just now."

"Oh no, not at all, there are so many. I only feel the big ones."

"Is this place new, this building?"

"Built in the 90s."

"How well will it hold up in a big earthquake?"

"That depends how big, I guess."

"Umm..."

I stared out the wall of glass, waiting for a follow-up. Outside, the city changed colours before my eyes. The roads flowed from grey, to pink, to purple, then disappeared into the horizon, swallowed by the sky. The roof of the Edo museum. A star in the night.

"Do you want to see what I brought?"

"Oh yes of course, obviously, sorry. I got caught up in the view. It's beautiful."

She turned to look out the windows.

"There's less humidity in the winter. You can see Mount Tsukuba in the distance."

She pulled a misshapen mass, white and reddish brown, from the backpack she was carrying. The fox from the other day. A part of it anyway. No tail, legs, or body. A head only. Limp and flat, ears folded back, canines bared, two gaping holes where its eyes once were. A head missing its skull. Suzuko grabbed it by the collar with both hands and I could tell the inside leather looked smooth. It was thin and flexible and light. It stretched like latex as Suzuko covered her head with it. Two faces one over the other. Their shapes complemented each other. A flash of beauty. Just for a moment. Because then Suzuko turned her back to me, her fingers on the back of her neck.

"Could you tie these laces here, please?"

Her voice was clear, natural. I tied the laces from the top of her head all the way to the base of her neck, making sure to stuff Suzuko's hair under the leather so it wouldn't stick out. The fox's hairs undulated between my fingers as I finished lacing.

175

"Pull tighter, please."

"I'm worried I'm going to hurt you."

"You won't hurt me."

I wrapped the laces around my fist so I could pull it tighter.

"A little tighter still, so so so, yes, like that."

Then she turned to face me and took my breath away.

White and red stripes for cheeks. The graceful muzzle. The ears long and pointy. The pelt glimmering in the light shining through the windows. Her eyes, surrounded by dark hairs, round and glistening.

"Oh that suits you so well!!!"

I felt an urge to throw myself at her but I didn't try anything, too stunned to move even a finger.

Sprawled on the futon. Her on top, me on the bottom. The light of a lamp dimmed by a piece of cloth. The curtains closed. Her body bare, light, delicate. Her fox head in the glittering darkness. Black nose in my neck. The fur of her cheeks. Her teeth biting the back of my left ear. Her gums. Drool. Thick and bloody strands. Clenching her jaw despite herself. I would have pushed her muzzle away from my neck but my wrists were tied. My ankles too. Tied to all four corners of the futon, while she panted, howled and bit even harder.

"Careful, that hurts."

But she clenched her teeth ever more furiously. Like trying to tear a steak out of a dog's mouth. She growled. I struggled in vain. Tightly bound. Suzuko pushing my shoulders against the futon with her hands. Or no, she wasn't. I hadn't noticed she was also wearing the fox's paws. Gloves, kind of, laced from the palm to the wrist. She must have slipped them on in the bathroom before coming to join me on the futon. Claws sharper than needles. She dug them into my shoulders and into my torso. She could have torn me in two if she'd wanted. But she only scratched me. Blood-red grooves slicing my skin into squares, swollen at the edges. I would have preferred she go easier on me. Or that she'd stop. But I said nothing. Her claws sank deeper and deeper into my flesh. Like raw chicken. That's the image I had in my mind. Exaggerating, of course. Everything would be ok. I'd heal quick. In any case, my love for her deepened with every nick and cut. My neck lacerated. Slobbery. Oozing. Her skin warm and moist. Rock hard, unavoid- able. Fear and desire. A wonderful combo. No other choice than to trust in her. She might kill me. Might not. Really what did it matter since I was with her? Suzuko. She didn't want to hurt me. It wasn't her fault, it was her claws. Her ges- tures were gentle otherwise. Or not. I couldn't think straight. I was bleeding a lot. From my neck, my shoulders, my torso, my belly. I didn't give a fuck. I was dying to kiss her, to slip my tongue between her teeth. The idea that she could rip it out of me. Her nose damp with a mixture of drool and blood. Thick and sticky. Her breath balmy. Her tongue in my mouth. Mine in her maw. As we rubbed ourselves against one another. She arched her back. Sweat and blood between her breasts. Suddenly I'm aware of it. The swaying of her hips. Our pubic hairs intertwined. Her protruding pelvic bone. Her ribs like the bones of a trout. And the fox, everywhere. Not just the head and paws. The whole body. The body of a delicate and supple and magnificently savage fox. Which I desperately wanted to caress. But my wrists, still strapped to the futon. I struggled with all my strength, then relaxed, then struggled again, until I managed to free one of my wrists. But I never got the chance to touch the fox's belly.

I woke up.

Suzuko's warm body lying against mine. The softness of her skin. The smell of damp leather. City light from behind the curtains. Her muzzle in my neck. I wasn't bound to the futon. She had fallen asleep wearing the fox head.

The next day Suzuko didn't take her fox head off at all. Or the day after. Or the day after the day after.

It took me a week before coming to terms with the fact that she had simply decided to wear the fox head around the apartment, and everywhere else. Nonstop. Day and night. She would walk the streets, wander through parks, she would go to the bar and cafés, to the restaurant and the cinema, to the museum and the grocery store. Always wearing her fox head. I remember at first she drew surprisingly little attention. People would look at her no differently than any other person walking by. Or they would casually look away as if to show her animal head was of no importance to them.

When we would go eat ramen near her place the server would talk to Suzuko about the heat and the late afternoon storms, the autumn he was hoping for and the winter whose name was better left unsaid (but which he complained about nonstop, no matter which season we were in). Suzuko would chat about the weather with the server while she waited for her bowl of ramen. When the bowl appeared on the counter in front of her, she'd separate the chopsticks with a snap before slurping up her noodles. When she was done she would wipe her muzzle with a napkin.

It was too cute.

I continued teaching English about twenty hours a week. And when I would leave the class Suzuko would sometimes be waiting for me on the sidewalk with Ayumi and we would go drink and eat in an izakaya in Roppongi or in Shinjuku. It was in one of these smoky dens that Ayumi suggested that Suzuko come perform in her gallery wearing her fox head. They freed up an evening, somewhere between the end of one exhibit and the setup for the next one, near mid-June.

The day of the performance, Suzuko wore capris, ordinary plastic flip-flops and a white t-shirt stuffed into her pants. We left her apartment together. The elevator. The lobby. The guard too absorbed by the incandescent glare of a screen to notice us pass by.

We retrieved our bikes from behind the building before taking the cycling path that runs along the canal to the Sumida River. Golden sun. Black water. To the left, towards the bridge that crosses to the other bank. On Shin-Ōhashi Avenue there were few cars in the streets. A few cyclists at the red lights. Suzuko. Her helmet crushing her ears but the fox's white and red muzzle still jutting out, clearly visible.

We turned left a few streets before the central train station, on Shōwa-dori, Ginza's main road, heading towards Ono Gallery.

Ayumi was waiting for us at the door. She and Suzuko went straight to the bar at the back of the gallery. And someone grabbed me by the shoulders. Pavle. I hadn't heard him arrive.

"Hi Vincent, how are you?"

"A little stressed, to be honest. There's so many people here... I thought this was going to be something small and informal, between two shows."

"Informal evenings don't exist in Tokyo."

"Oh I'll try to remember that..."

"Suzuko's last performance was a real hit, people want to see what she's presenting tonight."

"I can't wait to see it either."

"She hasn't told you what she's got up her sleeve?"

"No. And I have no idea if she's prepared anything. She hasn't gone to her workshop at all these past few weeks. We've been together this whole time... I half expected her to come teach English with me!"

No reaction from Pavle. Only half listening to me. His gaze fixed on the bar where Suzuko was chatting with Ayumi.

"She's magnificent..."

His voice dreamy.

"That fox head suits her so well... Ten years I've known her, Suzuko... and... it's crazy, it's like

I've always known her like that, with that head, I mean... It's... it's just *her*."

Pavle and I stood there awestruck, almost hypnotized, gazing at Suzuko at the other end of the gallery. Then she turned and walked towards us, her dark eyes glimmering like marbles, a large toothy smile flanking her mouth, and when she reached my left side she took my hand in hers and buried her muzzle in my neck for a moment. Since she started wearing the fox head on a permanent basis she'd allowed herself to show her affection for me no matter where we were.

One of Ayumi's assistants handed us some beers.

We drank them too fast.

A normal evening at the gallery, like any other. Diverse groups. Chatting. Drinking. Nothing exceptional. Nothing. Except that Suzuko was wearing a fox head. Two photographers snapping photos of her. But otherwise, most of the guests didn't need a second look. People came to see a performance but there was nothing to suggest they hadn't already seen the performance, or that they were seeing it now, or that they would see it later. In this kind of social setting, being a little blasé goes a long way. Nothing, though, could ever top the esthetics of what's-his-name's exhibit last December in Hanoi. Or so they said.

Honestly, we spent the evening, Pavle, Suzuko and I, drinking in a corner. Nothing particularly performative. And yet. I still had this feeling that there was in fact a performance. Somewhere. Here, elsewhere. That the world had changed, or that it was changing, or that it would change.

It wasn't even 8:30 when Suzuko and I left the gallery. She put on her helmet. I put on mine. I asked her if she wanted to come spend the night in my semibasement.

"No, why don't you just come live with me instead?"

"Is that offer a part of your performance?"

"Oh..."

She thought about it for a moment, the tip of her muzzle furrowed.

"Actually yes, Vincent, now that I think about it, it's true. The performance started well before we got to the gallery and will end well after. My life, our life, everything... it's all part of the performance now."

Newspaper articles about Suzuko, her fox head, the performance at Ono Gallery, began appearing in the weeks that followed. It didn't take long for the art critics to grasp that this wasn't just about performing in a gallery from time to time, but that, for Suzuko, her entire life would be the performance. If it had seemed, throughout the evening, like nothing much was happening, it was actually her way of showing there was no difference between the space inside the gallery and the space outside. And when there was no one around to see the performance, the show would still go on. It wasn't fundamentally new. But the contemporary art community in Tokyo began to take a greater—more sincere—interest in Suzuko's work, and in the up-and-coming gallery that represented her. Many artists, emerging and well established, were keen to draw Ayumi's attention to their practice. Applications literally began to pile up on her desk. Which was just as well, since Suzuko's performance didn't bring in a penny. If Ayumi wanted to financially support her friend's artistic process, she would have to increase the gallery's revenue. Which is why she chose to represent Aoshima Chiho, an interesting, fashionable artist who sold well too.

But never mind Aoshima Chiho.

In July, Tokyoites started following Suzuko when she would go for walks, live updating her route on online maps. It was thanks to this kind of blogging that Wada Kenji, a cultural journalist, first heard of Suzuko. There's very little news mid-summer to sink your teeth into. But with rumours of a woman wearing a fox head, he would go on to write the article of the season.

The photo of Arai Suzuko was published July 12, 2016 on the front page of *Asahi Shinbun*, a newspaper with a daily circulation of eight million copies.

And immediately people began staring at Suzuko when she would pass them on the street. The most daring would even try to take her picture, pretending to take shots of the city or a store's floral window display. And since we often went for walks together, they would take my picture too. Is that man her friend, boyfriend, husband? Bodyguard? Every blog had its own theory. Mostly, though, no one spent more time on me than was necessary. The reporters and the art historians, they only had eyes for Suzuko, and that suited me just fine. It was her performance, not mine.

It was Ayumi who dealt with the press most of the time. Suzuko preferred keeping the media as far away as possible. What she wanted was perfectly simple: to be left alone to live a normal life, wearing her fox head.

After a TV broadcast in Seoul, tourists from South Korea began pointing at Suzuko in the street, taking selfies with her, asking for her autograph. It was the first such broadcast outside of Japan to feature her. But not the last. Requests for interviews and photo shoots began streaming in. It wasn't easy to refuse them all. But that's what Suzuko wanted. Her popularity was already complicating her life outside the apartment. She would leave less often and for shorter periods. But it was counterproductive: her scarcity created enthusiasm. Every outing turned into a performative event.

Things were becoming more difficult.

The crowd of curious people grew by the day. And yet. There was no way Suzuko was going to take off her fox head. Soon enough summer would end. The tourists would go home. The media attention would die down. Soon there'd be better things to do than follow a woman in a fox head around Tokyo.

"I have to leave Japan soon, so I can renew my visa. It'd do us some good to see something different for a change, don't you think? I saw some cheap flights to Seoul for the beginning of August. You interested?"

We were sitting in our underwear on the balcony, cans of beer in our hands, after an entire day spent reading, cooking, making love. The city, scorching. Late afternoon, muggy.

"Oh yes it's true a change would be nice, but Korea, for me, that wouldn't be relaxing at all, seeing how Korean tourists react around me."

"You're right. Where should we go then? Singapore? I've never been."

I took a swig of beer. It was bubbly and cold.

"I'd really love to go with you but I can't."

"Bah... no worries. The next time I'll think about doing my visa stuff ahead of time, that'll give us some time to get organized."

"I don't think it will, no."

"Uhh..."

"Oh Vincent, I'm sorry... but... I can't leave Japan because... well, customs... you know, I'd have to take my fox head off and... that would be too sad... I don't want to."

Tears were forming in her eyes. I moved my chair closer to hers. Her arms damp. Her legs. Gently she slid her snout behind my ear. The moist fur of her muzzle. Her breath startlingly fresh. Her whiskers tickled my cheeks. Gave me goosebumps.

She stayed there a long time. Her muzzle nestled in my neck. She smelled good, of fur and leather. My fingers on her back. Drops of sweat racing down between her shoulder blades, the length of her spine, soaking the straps of her bra and the edges of her panties.

I traveled alone to South Korea to renew my visa.

And when I came back to Tokyo a week later, Suzuko was there in the airport waiting for me, standing in the middle of the arrivals hall. It had been a long time since she'd gone to such a busy place. A crowd had formed around her. I managed to find a way through. Suzuko. Hopping excitedly. I couldn't help but ruffle her fur, she was so cute.

"Oh stop!"

She was much happier than before I left. We boarded the train which took us from Narita to the central station and absolutely everyone in the car was staring at Suzuko. White cheeks. Black lips. Red around her eyes and forehead. Snout wide open. We sat beside each other and she rested her legs on my lap. Such a no-no on public transport. But she was doing it. The staring became more intense. She put her feet back down on the ground. She was smiling, looking sly, rolling my suitcase back and forth, squirming on the bench like she really had to go pee. A very strange performance.

"Vincent I've thought about this for a week, I really want to be able to travel outside of Japan with you and maybe one day go back to Montreal to meet your family and learn French (she was speaking quickly, forgetting to breathe) so I decided I'm going to get a passport with my fox head."

"Oh."

"What? Having a passport is part of a normal life, don't you think?"

"Yeah, sure."

"Eeeh! You don't think I can't get it?"

"Wait, no. I mean, yes. I haven't been thinking about it all week, like you. The idea just took me by surprise, that's all. And... well... I don't want to be a pessimist but... you'd have to convince the Japanese passport office and that's not going to be easy... Chances are, they're not the most progressive organization in the world."

She wrinkled her muzzle.

"Yeah, you're right. But, there it is, the next piece of my performance. I want the government to consider me a normal person."

"I find you perfectly normal."

"No I'm not! For you I'm extraordinary, obviously."

She put her legs back on my lap.

"Haha, you're going to have to choose. Either you're normal, or you're extraordinary."

"For you I'll be extraordinary and for the passport office I'll be normal!"

I was dying to ruffle her muzzle again.

"Listen to this. I started reading up a bit and... people who've changed their sex have managed without too much trouble to get a passport which reflects their new identity. Or women who widen their eyes, touch up their noses, inflate their lips, they also get new official documents, and easily too! You know, nowadays, thanks to biometrics, fingerprints, iris recognition software, customs agents around the world should easily be able to identify me. Oh! And I read something really interesting! A guy in Britain got a face transplant last year... And the UK just gave him a passport! Why couldn't I get one too, with my new head?"

Suzuko never wanted the media to be drawn to her fox head. It always made her feel uncomfortable, actually. But not any longer. Now she was going to use the media to get what she wanted.

From that point on she accepted every interview and would speak about only one thing: her intention to get a passport that reflected who she was in everyday life. If she could convince the rest of Japan, the government would have no choice. For her it was all about having the same rights as everyone else in society. Most of Japan's contemporary arts community got behind her. The director of the Tokyo National Museum of Modern Art even spoke out to proclaim that Japan, which prided itself on being at the forefront of the arts in Asia, was in danger of being outdone by neighbouring countries. It was a golden opportunity, before the Olympic Games kicked off, to show how open, modern, even how futuristic, the country was. Exactly the image Japan wished to project around the world.

But the passport office wasn't interested. An official document would never be issued to a woman, artist or not, who was wearing a fox head. That, at least, was what the Japanese foreign affairs minister repeated. On every platform.

Until South Korea offered Suzuko citizenship.

It wasn't a good look for Japan.

An envelope from the passport office arrived a year later on September 5, 2017. By registered mail. The postman held a screen out to Suzuko to confirm delivery. Then he looked embarrassed. He didn't step back, rummaging through his bag instead. He pulled a piece of cardboard out, some sort of two-legged fox drawn on it. Very childlike. In the background, what looked like the Eiffel Tower (the Tokyo Tower). Then the postman asked Suzuko, in an overly officious voice, if she would consent to append her signature to the bottom of the piece of cardboard as well.

Arai Suzuko.

The postman ceremoniously folded himself in half before retreating, slowly, stooping lower with every step, and thanking Suzuko a thousand times for having autographed his daughter's drawing. She was going to be over the moon—she wanted to be a fox now too.

Nothing new about young boys and girls wanting to change how they looked.

Together we sat on the futon. She looked serious. The hairs of her cheeks slightly on end. Her red and white ears standing to attention. Gazing gloomily. She tore at the envelope, took out the passport. A burgundy document marked with the imperial seal of Japan. She turned the booklet over and over again in her hand, hesitant. I held Suzuko against me. Then, delicately, she opened the passport to the first page.

"Oh look!"

Raining, outside, torrential, when Suzuko's phone started ringing.

"It's Ayumi, I'm going to answer it, ok?"

"Yeah, yeah, ok."

"Oha Ayumi... So so so... Of course but... Eeeh! You think so? Oh let me think about that for a bit... Yes, as soon as possible."

Then she hung up.

"What did she want?"

"She says that the National Museum of Modern and Contemporary Art in Seoul would like to see me perform."

"Where?"

"Eeeh! In Seoul, in one of their galleries!"

"Oh..."

Drops of rain angrily pelting the wall-to-ceiling windows. We sat up straight, backs against the wall, knees in our arms, at the head of the futon.

"What does Ayumi think?"

"I don't know. She was just relaying the message to me. I told her I'd think about it... But I'm going to say no. These performances, it's just my life, not something that plays out in a gallery. I thought everyone understood that!"

"People do understand, they just want to make a profit from you. It's perfectly fine if you turn down the offer if you don't want to do it."

The rain drops battered the windows with increasing ferocity. It was like hail.

"Oh Vincent, what I would like is to be able to live normally, like everyone else."

She was trembling.

"If you took off your fox head, people would look at you less, that's for sure."

"Eeeh! I can't do that!"

"Why not?"

"How... How could you love me, with my ordinary face?"

I laughed.

"I'm serious!"

"So am I! Honestly, you're funny."

She wrapped her arms around my neck. Fur gleaming. Eyes piercing.

"Is that what you would like, for me to take off my fox head?"

"No. I mean, not particularly."

Outside the rain was still coming down in torrents. She nestled her muzzle as she often did behind my ear. Her coat was silkier than usual. Her breath warmer. Her fangs sharper. My life could have ended there. I would have been perfectly happy.

"What if you surprised them a little, the museum in Seoul? We could go there and walk around like nothing was out of the ordinary. And we don't tell them beforehand. *That* would be the performance. Life. Just life."

"Oh I don't know."

"You fought so hard to get that passport, you should take advantage of it, even just a little bit, no?"

"Yeah... But... South Korea, I'm not sure I want to go there... What... what if we went to Montreal instead? I'd really love to see the bookstore where we met again. And that park with the squirrels... Could we do that?"

We bought two plane tickets for the following month. Landing in Montreal, October 4. When the fall colours would be at their fieriest. Or so we hoped.

While we waited, Suzuko went back to working in her workshop every day, which she hadn't done in months. Before leaving the apartment at dawn, she would leave me a little love letter on the bedside table. And when she would get home late afternoons, she wouldn't say a word about what she did during the day at the workshop. She would only tell me which path she took to get there, as if the destination served no purpose.

She was preparing a performance piece. I could feel it.

Her anxiety. The way her heart kind of skipped. And the way she looked at the city. The glimmer of morning. Golden reflections. She marvelled at them. At the crack of dawn. Out on her bike. Enjoying the ride. She would have loved for her life to be made up entirely of these kinds of anonymous trips. Cycling between the river and the Tsukiji fish market. As people went about their business, loading and unloading containers, without paying her the slightest heed.

The fish market takes up an enormous amount of space. A city in the city. Lively early mornings, dead in the afternoons.

There was no guarantee that Canadian customs would accept Suzuko's Japanese passport. To reassure myself I made an appointment at the Canadian embassy. An austere building surrounded by a stone garden. Aoyama Avenue. A stone's throw from the cemetery of the same name. And to my great surprise the ambassador himself, Ian Burney, came to meet me. A thin, greying man. Buck tooth and metal glasses. He'd been informed (by who knows which intelligence agency) that Arai Suzuko had bought herself a ticket to Montreal. He wanted to personally reassure me that she'd be able to enter the country without any problems, as per the agreements in place between Canada and Japan. We should, however, expect a little welcoming committee at the airport. A few reporters. A few politicians. A few curious onlookers. Possibly a brief handshake with Justin Trudeau since he'd be passing through Quebec early October.

Obviously this kind of attention would be an annoyance to Suzuko, who would have preferred to arrive incognito in Montreal. But I'd been blindsided. The ambassador opened the door for me and politely invited me to step out of his office.

I left the embassy with an unpleasant feeling.

For a moment I stood motionless outside the stone garden. Pebble grooves. Three slender monoliths. Islands in a sea of grey. Then I went back into the building to ask that they let Suzuko enter the country in peace but no one was available to meet with me anymore. I would have to make another appointment.

I went into the cemetery next to the embassy. I rode around, trying to work out how best to convince the ambassador to let Suzuko travel to Canada without all the fuss. Slowly I rode straight up the main path, paved, flat, and lined with headstones of varying sizes, fearing that, for Suzuko, everything would be the same in Montreal as it was in Tokyo, that reporters would get carried away with themselves, that people would hound her in the streets, that they'd keep her from a normal existence. She wore a fox head. They'd never leave her in peace because of it.

A few tailless cats scampered across the cemetery paths. I rode. Tailless cats pouncing from headstone to headstone. Hmmm... I once read that, during the Edo period, cats would have their tails cut off so they wouldn't be caught by evil spirits. I mulled that over in my mind. And I rode. Trying to delay as much as possible the moment I'd have to go back to the apartment and tell Suzuko about the kind of welcome she should expect in Montreal.

I hopped off my bike. Leaned it against a tree. And started wandering the cemetery walkways. Maybe we should cancel our trip to Montreal. The midday heat. Parched grass. A woman wearing a yukata, her back bent over, her face sagging.

"Good afternoon, ma'am."

She raised her eyebrows and all the skin in her face rose with it. A facelift of sorts, which offered a quick glimpse of the girl she was in her twenties. She placed a hand on a tomb. Looking exhausted.

"Do you need a hand?"

"No thank you, I only come here to feed the cats."

Her voice was clear and confident. To hear her, it was obvious she didn't need any help, despite the tattered yukata she wore, the broad, half frayed belt, the flimsy hemp strap barely holding her big toes in her getas. A filthy headscarf in her hair. A FamilyMart plastic bag dangling from her arm. And a horde of cats circling her with excitement. Although the woman didn't seem in any rush to feed them.

"Sorry to ask, but... I heard there was once a time when people would cut the tails off of cats to stop evil spirits from possessing their bodies. Do people still cut the tails off cats, nowadays, in Tokyo?"

She raised her eyebrows, revealing once again, for a moment, the youthful features of a young woman, before her face caved back in on itself as if in a landslide.

"Of course not! That'd be animal cruelty!"

"Then why don't any of the cats around you have any tails?"

She took a fish head out of the FamilyMart bag. She tossed it in front of her. Three cats and two crows flung themselves at it. The woman kicked the crows, chasing them off. The three cats fought, meowing and hissing, until one of them managed to make off with the fish head.

"You know cats have nine lives, right?"

"Uhh... no..."

"And so they have nine tails too. They grow one after the other."

"Ah ok..."

"The cats you see here have used up all of their lives, and so all of their tails too. To outrun death they live here, in the cemetery. They're starving. I feed them."

Then she tossed another fish head in the grass.

When I got back to the apartment Suzuko was still out. September 15, 2017. Wall of windows. Waning day. Artificial glimmer. I was thinking about our trip to Montreal, about Suzuko wanting to revisit the places where we met. When two police officers knocked at the door.

"Are you the husband of Arai Suzuko?"

"We aren't married, but we live together. What's the problem?"

"There was an accident near the river, behind the fish market. It's forbidden to ride a bike there, it's dangerous, she was hit by a reefer truck."

Legs weak.

"Is she ok?"

"Don't worry, yes, she's fine. An ambulance took her to the hospital. We can take you there, if you'd like."

I found myself sitting in the backseat of a small police car. Don't worry, yes, she's alright.

That's what they were telling me, confidently. But what did they really know, these two police-men? Slowly we drove. I wished they'd turn on their flashing lights and hurry up. If things were critical, that's what we'd be doing, so they mustn't be critical, then. That's what I kept telling myself to keep calm. Pedestrians overtaking us. I should have gone on my bike. I wanted to kick my door open, run to the hospital. But which hospital was it, again? Did they even tell me? We should have taken the overpass instead of winding our way through these tiny streets. An interminable line of red lights. A new day. Packed sidewalks. An ambulance. The hospital.

The police officers wished me luck.

At the reception desk I asked where I could find Arai Suzuko's room. The receptionist smiled at me, reassuringly.

"Oh Arai Suzuko, she was admitted no more than two hours ago."

All was well. Just a minor injury.

"Wait here, please, someone will come get you in a moment."

I sat down in an almost deserted room. On a chair. Back to the wall. Polished floor. Suspended ceiling.

Then a young doctor came. He led me to his office. Where he told me Suzuko was dead.

Later.

I followed the doctor through a hallway. White and empty. The sound of our footsteps lingering on the waxed floor. The elevator. In silence. Fourth floor. Another hallway. Empty and suffocating. Vision wavering. Not a drop of saliva left. No legs left to walk on.

"Here we are."

"What?"

"The room."

I entered.

On the table next to the bed was a transparent plastic bag. Inside, keys, wallet, a phone that suddenly began to vibrate. It paraded around in the bag like a living being. Suzuko. Things in a transparent bag. A call. A bag. Things. The bed. The body under a white sheet. The fox head. Soiled and flattened. On the table. Next to the bag. Suzuko. I didn't dare ruffle her muzzle. It looked limp. It looked dead.

I stepped closer to the bed. I desperately needed someone to support me. A shape under the sheet. Suzuko's human face. More than a year since I'd last seen it. Barely remembered it. I hesitated. Three minutes or three hours. Then I pulled back the sheet. My eyes closed. Then I opened them. And I saw. Her moist, oily skin. Her naturally white neck. Her ears, as fine as roses. Her flat hair. Her pale lips.

And her eyelids.

Blood-red eyelids. Glowing like the setting sun. A glossy vermilion line surrounding them, as if the edges had been cut with a scalpel. Eyelids. They devoured her forehead and cheeks. The impact of the accident. The truck's bumper. Eyelids. Only. Like I've never seen. Thick and weeping. Magnificent and terrible. Eyelids that would certainly, forever, haunt me.

QC FICTION

Current & Upcoming Books

Visit **qcfiction.com** for details and to subscribe
to a full season of QC Fiction titles.